THE ALPHA DRACULA

THE ALPHA DRACULA

Raymond Boyd

To order additional copies of this book, contact:
Xlibris
844-714-8691
www.Xlibris.com
Orders@Xlibris.com
610986

Dedicated to

ILIAS LOUIE HARAKIDAS

Date of birth: March 14, 1949
Date of death: September 22, 2004

ACKNOWLEDGMENTS

Thanks to the encouragement of my dear wife Gloria. It was her belief that I have the ability to write a story that has intrigued many who have enjoyed the countless writings and movies as well as stage productions of the immortal Count Dracula.

My sincere gratitude to my daughter Paula Boyd for always acknowledging that there is a story in my writing.

I would like to thank:

NORMA TISA
MARCELLA McCALL
JO ANN BRERLEY
ANITA LEO
JOAN MITCHELL
BARBARA CRAWFORD
NEVIN LONG
BEN FISHER
BRIAN DERAGO
BUD TOMLINSON
STEVE WOOD
TOMMY & EVON HARAKIDAS
PERRI & FAMILY HARAKIDAS
FRANK BELLOCCHIO
JANNY KAFKIAF

Contents

PREFACE

So was he born; the product of the lust for eternal life. Through the centuries evil has walked the earth in it's human form of Count Dracula. This is the factual account of the birth and apparently the never ending existence of the sperm of Satan and Zanza; the woman that conceived and brought life to him. Francis; the young monk, who came to Transylvania to rid his doubt of his worthiness to serve the holy order. Destiny would decide his dilemma after his encounter with Dracula.

After several centuries, in 1521, Pope Clement VII crossed paths with the immortal count, and unknowingly preserved the Holy See.

In the year 1803 he was found in Napoleon's France and Josephine's bed. Although historians do not record it I have found documental proof that he engineered Napoleon's Waterloo in his quest to rule the world.

Also contained in these writings are the answers to the questions that have plagued the quizzical mind of man. How had he obtained his physical powers of metamorphoses? His revulsion for wine? Why, although he is of solid substance, he casts no reflection? His vulnerability to fire? Why is he repelled by the cross or the Holy Eucharist? How did he achieve immortality? Why have generations of the Von Helsing family pursued him over half the European Continent?

This is the story of the people who attempted to put an end to his murderous rapes and bloodletting. The woman who caused a change of direction in his life; Zanza, the mother whom he would come to love hundreds of years later.

Lady Lispeth; the woman he would take after death.

Lady Isabella; he offered her immortality.

Jeanean Purkinjie; who travelled to Transylvania in search of him, only to find him in France, calmly waiting for her.

Dr. Kurt Von Helsing; who had a quest for the destruction of Dracula and that would result in an alliance.

I know he still lives! For during the course of my research for this book, I have matched wits with him and was fortunate enough to escape with my life. But that is another story!

Raymond Boyd

PROLOGUE

In the year of our Lord 1900, I have moved in hiding into this lovely countryside of Cardiff, England. I take a pen and paper in order to put my findings of forty years, collecting the evidence that I have gathered in my travels throughout the European continent. I have just completed the translation of the last manuscript from French into the King's English. I pray for God's protection to complete the task to alert mankind of the existence of he who feeds on humanity. Ten days have passed since I have had food or drink in the hope to purge my soul and mind of the sins of my life. Night after night, for the past four days, after the sun leaves the heavens, it has been increasingly difficult to maintain sufficient heat in my small cottage. I know he is outside my door, as the odor of sulphur seeps into my abode. I am certain that had I not obtained and placed the Holy Eucharist by my door, my death would have been imminent. Nevertheless, I shall press on. The story of his handiwork must be told. The world must be warned of the existence of Count Dracula. Three days from this day, I will be eighty years of age. I, John-Paul, have left the monastery the order of St. Francis of Assisi. I have informed my solicitor by post to visit me on my eightieth birthday. I have left instructions for the wording on my headstone, which is "John-Paul, the Apostle."

Also, the solicitor is charged with the obligation of publishing this manuscript. As instructed, the solicitor arrive at the cottage. The body still warm to the touch. His death must have been pleasant, he mused, as he looked down on the smiling face. If you are reading this, then it is evident that he has discharged his duties to the letter.

CHAPTER 1

SATAN'S PROMISE

Yes, it is the truth: I am the ruler of both the light and dark world; what you petition is mine to give, Your homage has pleased me; eternal life you shall have, "SATAN LIES." Elated, Val dropped to his knees and kissed Satan's feet. Instantly, Val's lips burned and blistered. It took all his self-control to suppress the scream from emitting. Satan then instructed Val to go and lay with Zanza; henceforth, she will give birth to a son. "Through him you shall have everlasting life. We are finished," Satan said and disappeared.

Zanza lived alone deep in the forest in a log cabin connected to a cave at the base of a mountain. There she worshipped and copulated periodically with Satan since the age of twelve. "It is the master's wish that I lay with you," Val related, the tone of his voice clearly full with anticipation. His eyes expressed his lust. Val rid himself of his garments as he spoke. Zanza also removed hers. "Come and lay here," Zanza said, pointing to a large stone table, and as Val did so, Zanza slowly walked to the fireplace that had been hewed and removed a wooden cup and dipped it into an iron pot that sat on slow-burning coals containing a thick brown liquid. "Drink this," she offered, and without question, Val accepted. Zanza explained that after he consumed it, he would experience a euphoric sensation.

He greedily gulped it down as his eyes consumed Zanza's nakedness. Instantly Val lapsed into a deathlike sleep that lasted seventy-two hours.

He awakened both elated and exhausted with no memory of what transpired. As he slowly focused on his surroundings, he thought it strange that he could not recall having possessed this voluptuous naked creature that stood before him.

Zanza stood five feet three inches tall and weighed one hundred thirty pounds, with waist-length blond hair that framed her oval-shaped face. Her emerald eyes seemed to pierce into one's soul, and her facial features were evenly matched. Although her smile was beguiling, Val could not resist a feeling of apprehension. Suddenly the impulse to ravish her overcame him, and his attempt to take hold of her was rebuffed. She commanded that he go and not return until he was summoned. Zanza's tone of voice caused Val to remain motionless and bewildered. Seething, Val resisted the impulse to take hold of Zanza by her throat and squeeze the life out of her. Wordless, he turned on his heels and departed. "Be assured I have conceived the seed of life," she loudly proclaimed as Val hurriedly made his exit. He mounted his horse, and the moment he spurred his steed, he was aware that Zanza was not alone. He clearly heard the distinctive, maniacal laughter from Zanza's abode. Unnerved, he galloped without abandon through the dangerously dense woods. It had been ten days that Val had been away. The order was given to lower the drawbridge as Val approached the moat. The captain of his guards greeted him, but Val did not return his greeting. He instead gave orders that he was not to be disturbed as he hastened to his chambers. His servant attempted to remove Val's clothing as was customary, but that effort was rebuffed. Val did manage to remove his boots before he staggered to his bed fully clothed. He then lapsed into a forty-eight-hour, deathlike sleep.

The title "Magnificent" he bestowed upon himself was jealousy guarded. Val had no living relatives, and days before his twenty-first birthday, he had conceived the plan that no relative would lay claim by birthright to his title and sovereignty. The simplicity of his dilemma caused him to convulse hysterically into laughter. On his birthday he commanded people to attend his celebration to "feed, fornicate, and kill them." They numbered sixty-four women, ninety-seven men, fifty-five children—all totaled to two hundred sixteen. The festivity climaxed three weeks later. All through the night as they slept, all were systematically murdered. Val watched with glee as his assailant cut their throats, and for many, he had ordered their hearts cut out.

It was six months from the day that Val had bargained with the prince of darkness, as he prepared to retire, the sound of wings alerted him as they beat against the window. Cautiously, he approached, astonished that he was momentarily gripped with fear as he gazed at the sight of a bat several times larger than any he had ever seen before. Instinctively, Val was aware that he was being summoned by Zanza. Three days later, Val arrived without an escort at Zanza's abode. Val slowly dismounted and entered. Not acknowledging his presence, Zanza continued to suckle the infant she held to her breast. She had conceived and delivered as was foretold. She announced with pride, without looking at Val, that the master is pleased. Val replied it has only been six months since he had lain with her and asked why he had been compelled to be there. "What have I to do with that you have spawned?" The placenta was still dripping from between her legs as she slowly arose from the chair, naked. Angrily, Zanza replied, "The boy could no longer wait in my belly; behold his alluring consonance."

Ten minutes before Val arrived, Satan had appeared. The moment Zanza gave birth, he came at her side and removed the infant from between her legs with the umbilical cord still attached, raised it above his head in a thundering voice, and proclaimed, "My son shall subsist on the blood of your creatures." He then returned the child into the outstretched arms of his mother to be suckled. "What shall he be called, my Prince?" Satan ignored the question and raised his eyes upward and boomed, "Your son has said his blood was offered for the salvation of mankind, but my son shall have power beyond mortal men, and his dealings with them will be draconian." A black cloud engulfed Satan as he cast his eyes downward and said, "All shall know of him as Dracula." Taken aback by the stench, Val found it difficult to breathe as he entered Zanza's abode. He was acutely aware that Satan had preceded his arrival. He approached Zanza as she lay naked, cradling the sleeping child, and without bothering to look at Val, Zanza spoke softly, saying, "Behold the son of the great one, you are to leave now and henceforth twelve years from this day.

It has been commanded by the great one that you be given charge of our son at that time." Quickly Val turned and departed without response. He was greatly relieved that Zanza had not given him the care of the suckling. He was also bewildered by Zanza's declaration, "Son of the great one." His dismay was quickly resolved as he reasoned that is it not so that I am "Val the Magnificent?"

Val was pleased as he considered himself fortunate that he had not encountered Satan upon his arrival. He had bedded Zanza as he was told; now all that remained was for him to contemplate on his immortality. Although elated that he successfully bargained with the prince of darkness, he was plagued by the fact he had to impregnate the witch. Could there be some underlying motive? If so, what can it be?

Zanza had been instructed by Satan to educate Dracula who had proven to be an apt pupil. He mastered languages, literature, history, as well as mathematics. His primary interest was in the dogmas of religion—Judaism, Catholicism, Hinduism, Paganism, and Islam. The twelve years rapidly concluded, and as Zanza attempted to explain why their time together must end, without warning, Dracula slapped her face. The impact knocked her down, and as she lay stunned, Dracula knelt beside her, sneering, and asked, "Do you not know that I am aware that the time is near for me to do my father's bidding?" "Yes, yes," she stammered. Zanza's love for her son was only surpassed by her devotion and insatiable love for her lord and master "Satan."

In the twelve years Zanza spent nourishing and teaching Dracula, he did not feel emotionally bound to her and was completely devoid of affection toward her. On Dracula's twelfth birthday, Zanza, with her son in hand, arrived at Val's castle. "What is your business here?" asked one of the two soldiers shouting down from the guard tower. Zanza looked upward, making eye contact with him, and without further challenge, he felt compelled to release the lock and put into motion the lowering of the drawbridge. Several minutes later, Zanza and Dracula were escorted to the great hall where Val held court. Wordless, they stood for one hour before Val appeared. His displeasure was obvious as he asked, "Is he now twelve years of age?" Zanza ignored the question and simply announced that she would return in twenty-one years to reclaim him. Without further ado she departed.

Val felt contemptuous of Zanza's lack of respect and would have imprisoned her and personally stripped the skin off her body had it not been for the fact that she had the favor of Satan. He then turned his attention to the boy and looked with disdain as he thought it odd that there was not a likeness of himself, although Dracula's expression was bland. Val sensed that the boy was equally contemptuous of him and signaled to the captain of his guards that had been standing at attention by the door twenty feet away. As he approached within five feet of his sovereign, Val scornfully ordered him to take charge of the waif and be sure to keep him from his sight. Furthermore, he asked him to see if he has the aptitude for battle. Val then briskly walked away. Some minutes later, he entered his bedchambers, and as he stood in front of a six-foot four-inch mirror with the memory of the face of the boy, he agreed with his assumption that there was no likeness of himself in the boy. He then pondered Zanza's departing words that she would return in twenty-one years to claim her son. Several minutes elapsed as Val continued to look at his reflection. He was disturbed by the obvious fact that he was looking older. How could this be? He had kept his part of the pact with Satan. Would he not do the same? Distraught, Val remained concealed for a week in drunken stupor. Captain Yago had been a general and statistician, and it was he who should have been given credit for Val's success in battles. Yago had been kicked in the head by his own horse while drunk. He was attempting to put his mount through a series of jumps. The incident resulted in a momentary lapse of memory. Val's first thought was to execute him, but if he had done so, he feared his army would rebel against him. Val was well aware that his army was loyal to the general; hence, he reduced him in rank. Dracula did learn much from Captain Yago. It was primarily the tactical art of war, and to not show any mercy to the vanquished. He explained that if you give mercy, they would have the opportunity to engage you again in battle. Captain Yago's teaching was to no avail. Dracula's only interest was the pleasure of the flesh. Dracula grew six feet tall, with hazel eyes, which when angry, transformed the pupils into a piercing black. The effect to an observer was frightening; otherwise women found him intriguing and charming, and men felt in awe of him. Val's resentment toward Dracula as he saw him over the passing years grew strong as he himself became weaker and rapidly getting older. At the age of fifteen, Val sent Dracula to distant lands with his army to pillage and bring back prisoners. Val had given orders to the commander of his army to be sure that Dracula was to be placed at all time in the foremost position of all battles. Val was confident that Dracula would be killed or captured. The fates had deemed it to be not so. Dracula refused to participate in future battles, and on his thirtieth birthday, he traveled to France and introduced himself upon his arrival as Count Dracula. He took residence in a chateau located on the outskirts of Paris, and this purchase quickly brought him to the attention of aristocracy. Dracula entertained lavishly, and many of the nobles curry his favor. The two and a half years that Dracula had been away, Val had watched himself growing old and worried that something was amiss. He was sixty-two years of age, but he had the face and body of a man of eighty-five years. Val failed in attempts to contact Satan for the past ten years, nor could he find Zanza to solicit her aid in summons to Satan. Val ceased to enjoy the cries and screams of those he had impaled and begging for mercy. He now reasoned in his twisted mind that the problem lay with the birth of Dracula. Val recalled the words spoken almost thirty-three years ago by Satan, "You will have everlasting life through a son." So therefore, Val reasoned that if he destroyed Dracula and offered him unto Satan, he would cease to age. He determined the time of the offering to be in six months, on Dracula's thirty-third birthday. On the pretense of celebrating Dracula's birthday, Val would offer a feast to be held in Dracula's honor. Poison would be the method for the guest of honor's demise.

CHAPTER 2

THE OATH

Orloff and Boris were brothers who lived with their families in Transylvania all of their lives. They were not brave men, just simple peasant stock. They lived in constant fear as they tended their small farms with their families. Orloff, the older of the two, had fathered nine children, and there now only remained five. Boris had eleven, and now only six remained. Their children's fate had all been the same; they all simply vanished without a trace. Of course, the disappearance of children was not rare in this small country. The same cursed event had befallen scores of families for the past several generations.

Orloff and Boris did not search for their lost children because they knew it would be fruitless, for no missing child had ever been found. The brothers agreed that the evil one, Zanza, was the cause. Now, twenty years after, they both suffered the same accursed misfortune. The last disappearance was just two days ago, when Boris' seven-year-old child would be the last victim—so they swore. Now with one day before Dracula's thirty-third birthday, Zanza had much to do. She looked to where the small boy lay, where he had been placed by her two days ago. She forced liquid into him. The drug paralyzed him, but he remained alert.

Dracula returned from France, his stay being interrupted by a message sent from Val to return at once. He wondered why the message was so urgent. He had been away from home many times before and thought it unusual for his father to summon him after ignoring his existence. Dracula only obeyed out of curiosity and partly because he was tiring of the young noblemen and ladies he had been entertaining. He arrived home in the morning of his thirty-third birthday. Val greeted him and suggested he should rest after his long journey, because guests would be arriving shortly. Dracula asked what this had to do with him. Val replied that he arranged a marriage of states with the king of Romania. The bride-to-be was the king's niece. He stated furthermore that the alliance would secure the protection of Transylvania's borders. Dracula knew that this was a command and, therefore, was not debatable, and though he did not fear his father, he offered no objection. He never intended to take a wife and mused to himself that this alliance could prove to be quite amusing. Furthermore, he could always rid himself of the wench when he tired of her. Upon hearing what Val had to say, his first thought had been to summon his coachman and immediately depart. The two men held each other's eyes for a few seconds. Val, for the first time, looking into the cold hazel eyes of his son, felt a sense of recognition. He did not dwell on it, because he was too consumed with the elaborate scheme that he had contrived for the murder of his son. Dracula, seeing only the excitement in Val's eyes, felt a wave of apprehension but dismissed it. They then turned and took leave of each other.

CHAPTER 3

DEATH BY POISON

With only hours remaining, Zanza began preparing the now-horrified boy for his demise. She removed the dagger from the hot coals where she had placed it a half hour ago. It now glistened with a reddish hue that seemed to be almost transparent. The naked boy stared in mute silence as Zanza began cutting from the boy's navel by drawing the blade four inches upwards.

She now removed the half-crazed and starved rat from its cage and placed her fingers into the wound, lifting the bloody flesh where she inserted the rat. The boy could only hear his own screams inside of his head as the rat ate vigorously. In less than two minutes, the boy swallowed his tongue and died. She then removed the now-bloated animal and returned it to its cage. The body was then taken and fed to the equally half-starved swine. She was well pleased with herself; the ritual was almost complete. Now it was time to claim the body of Dracula.

Had Dracula been aware that there only remained two hours of his life, he surely would have torn out the heart of his father. Dracula had consumed his fifth cup of wine after Val poured the deadly drops of poison. One hour had passed; he knew only two more hours were left to the life of his son. Dracula, of course, had his own plan, though not as sinister or deadly as his father's; his only thoughts were to consummate his engagement to the king's niece, while he poured cup after cup of drink into the old king.

Lady Lispeth, at nineteen, was even more than Dracula hoped for. Lispeth, in turn, was completely mesmerized by Dracula's magnetic charm. She felt compelled to yield to his oblivious desires, knowing fully well what they were. Unbeknownst to him, however, was the old king's tolerance for drink. In three more hours' time, Dracula would have succeeded, but unfortunately, he himself would be dead within the next twenty minutes. Val's calculation proved correct. While still laughing, Dracula suddenly slumped forward on the table, his chair sliding from behind as he fell to the floor, dead.

Val, walking calmly, bent and placed his hand upon the breast of his now-dead son. Hardly able to conceal his delight, he announced to the guest that the shadow of death had befallen his house. Lady Lispeth, having recovered after being attended by her handmaiden, sat pale and trembling, as she and her uncle listened in shock as Val commanded that the feast continue, explaining it would have been the wish of his son. The forty other guests were delighted. Val had but one more thing to do in the morning, and that was to cut out the heart of his son.

Zanza, having slipped into the castle, walked where only minutes before the servants had placed the body of Dracula. With little or no effort, she placed the corpse in her cart and departed. After she arrived at her dwelling, she worked swiftly.

CHAPTER 4

KILL THE WITCH

The brothers, Orloff and Boris, bid farewell to their families, it now being first light. Their journey would take three days and three nights. They had decided to destroy, forever, the woman known as Zanza. Such an undertaking would require the blessing of the holy one who lived in the Carpathian Mountains. The sun offered little warmth on this bitter, cold morning as they set forth. This was the first time either man had shown any form of courage, because they had a feeling of determination. But if they were aware that only one would return, they would have remained sheepish.

Zanza again removed the now-contented rat from its cage and leaned over the body. She turned the head to the left, exposing the throat, and then placed the head of the rat on the jugular vein, knowing that the greater part of the blood that had circulated in the head, face, and neck would return to the throat. As the rat bit, Zanza applied pressure to its spine, causing the rat to inject its fluid. Then removing the now—dead rat, she cut its belly open and allowed the blood to pour into the mouth of Dracula. The ritual was now complete, and there only remained two small punctures on the throat of Dracula. His lips quivered, the eyes fluttered; he was alive. Zanza quickly expressed the urgency to make haste, for the sun would be up within the hour. The place she chose for him was a small cave not far from hers. Zanza then explained the need for him to avoid, at all costs, the daylight hours; not doing so would be certain disaster to him. In the cave, she had placed a coffin with one inch of soil inside. "Here you will sleep the sleep of the undead during the daylight hours. Remember all that I have taught you as a boy. All else will come to you as you sleep." Dracula lowered himself into his coffin and pulled the lid shut. With the taste of blood still in his mouth, he knew fully well that he would soon have more. Zanza returned to her dwelling to give thanks to her lord and master. Little did she know she would soon join him in hell.

The old monk bade farewell to the two visitors, promising to pray for them. He knew that the poor souls did not understand that he could not give his blessing for the taking of a life, no matter what the circumstance. When the brothers had finished relating to him their mission, he told them to leave the matters in the hands of God and return to their homes and pray.

This they could not do, for the hatred imbedded in their very souls to carry out this act of vengeance would not allow them to heed his advice. Did they think he did not understand their suffering and grief? Should he have told them of the burden he himself bore these many years? As a young man, he and his father lived in a small village, his mother having died giving birth to him. His father would never take another wife but devoted all his love to his son and his most profitable business as a merchant. His father had given him the name Paul, from the Holy Book. He had been sent to Bucharest for his education. At the age of eighteen, as planned, he returned to Transylvania to help his father. However, fate interfered, and two weeks after he arrived home, Paul met and married Marie.

Marie's father was Ukrainian, and her mother, a gypsy. Her parents were put to death for practicing witchcraft. Marie, along with Kavik, the leader of the cult, fled with no time to spare. They traveled from Balkans to Transylvania. They arrived one year before Paul returned and purchased a small farm on the first day of their arrival. The sellers, with their two small children, were never seen again. This was the beginning of the disappearances of the young ones. Marie, at twenty, was five feet one inch tall, with waist-long black hair, olive complexion, and haunting green eyes and was a stronger contrast to Kavik's apelike appearance. At well over two hundred sixty pounds, five feet nine inches tall with dark animal-like brown eyes, Kavik looked much older than his fifty years.

The small farmhouse was ideal for their purposes, but they did not work the land. In truth, from the day that they set foot on the land, it ceased to yield. Kavik taught Marie all that he knew of the art of black magic. The one thing Kavik was unable to accomplish was direct contact with the demon. This, Marie would do on her own after Kavik's death. Paul remembered the first time he saw her buying supplies in his father's store. It was his first day back. He thought that he had never seen one so beautiful. Her only thought was the need for his sperm. This service Kavik could not perform for her. Paul's father opposed when told of his intent to take Marie as his wife. He begged him to put the silly notion out of his head. "But you have not seen her, Father," Paul cried. Marie returned the next day. This time Paul spoke to her and told her of his intention to make her his bride. Marie encouraged him by telling him of her desire to see him again. This she did, and within two weeks, they were wed. The day before the wedding, Paul's father pleaded with him not to go through with it, telling him he saw a great evil in her. Paul explained that no matter what his father said, he would have this woman as his wife. Paul will never forget the tears in his father's soft blue eyes. Till this day, Paul continued to pray for his father's forgiveness. Marie was aware of his father's opposition to their union. However, she did not feel threatened, because her plans had been well thought out. Paul's father would be among the dead within the year.

Paul had no memory of the first nine months that he spent with Marie. He felt that he lived in a gray mist, full with shadows. His first clear memory was hearing the cry of an infant. As he walked into the room, he saw Kavik placing the child in a pail of blood. He watched in shock as the child was then taken out of the pail and put on the filthy cot. He then saw Marie and Kavik drink and wash themselves with the bloody liquid. As he turned to flee, he saw their eyes lift and gaze at him with mock amusement as he ran out of the house. The sound of great laughter followed him, and he realized there was another one in the house.

Filled with fear, he arrived at his father's house, only to be met by terrifying screams from within. The physician saw at once that Paul was in shock and forced a vial of tiny substance into Paul's parched mouth. Within a few minutes, Paul was in deep sleep. Twenty-four hours later, he awoke and listened as his father's old friend and doctor explained his hopelessness and his inability to save his dear friend. The good doctor tried to prepare Paul for what he was about to see. But how could he? He himself, after two days in attendance, could not accept what his own eyes beheld. He knew his efforts would be in vain. All he could advise was for him to pray to God for strength as he led him to his now-quiet and dying father.

When he walked into his father's bedroom, he saw the old housekeeper on her knees in silent prayer by the bed. As he stepped closer, he saw that his father lay naked and tied. He started to turn to the doctor for an explanation but then saw what it was that the doctor could never explain. As though appearing to grow out of the stomach were swarming wormlike creatures that, in reality, were eating their way out. Paul felt the hands of the doctor on his shoulders, leading him out of the room. He heard the soft voice announce that his father was now with God.

The following morning, Paul buried his father and vowed to avenge his death. He somehow knew that Marie bore the responsibility for the murder and horrible death that his father had suffered. Before he could return to destroy the evil that befell Transylvania, he had been told by the old housekeeper that another child had disappeared. When he returned to the little farmhouse, he found no one there. He entered and went to Kavik's room where he knew he had witnessed a ritual. He also found one small shoe. Now Paul realized whose blood had been in the pail. His eyes were drawn to a jar, which held the same cannibal worm that had devoured his father. If only he had stood in this very room only a week before to hear Marie instruct

Kavik to take the female worm to the house of her father-in-law and place it by the sleeping man's ear, whereupon it would enter to hatch her eggs deep into the man's stomach. If only he could have saved his father from such horror.

As Paul left to seek them out, he picked up the sharp stained axe. Within a few minutes, he came upon the three of them. Marie and Kavik were on their knees, with the infant facedown between them. Marie was feeding the flames with the lower and last half of the kidnapped boy. She intoned that this would be their offering of thanks to their winged god. They did not see or hear until, as if in warning, a cry came from the infant. Paul raised the axe and, with all his strength, brought it down. As she turned to face him, her mouth opened, but the only sound that came was the steel splitting the bone from the forehead and lodging in the bridge of the nose. Kavik picked up the infant and cried to Paul, "Would you kill your own child?" As Paul struggled to free the axe, he looked toward Kavik holding the child.

His arms became weak, and he released the handle of the bloody axe. His voice, clear and strong, ordered Kavik to take that thing from hell and go. Even as he spoke, he knew the child was evil, but he could not bring himself to kill it. Kavik fled into the woods, holding the child and reaffirming his devotion to his master for the privilege of having to care for the baby, Zanza. Kavik would be dead at the hands of his ward in fifteen years. Paul placed Marie's body with the axe still in place on the fire and asked her master to receive it. Now, after these many years in the monastery, once again, with the coming of the two men asking for his blessing to take the life of his own daughter, he still was not sure if he had done the right thing in sparing her life. Paul cried out to God for forgiveness for his weakness and the great sin he had committed so long ago. He also asked God to protect and forgive the two brothers.

Orloff and Boris were waiting when Zanza returned. Boris was hiding on the roof over the door, and Orloff was inside. As Zanza approached within five feet of the entrance, Boris leaped down onto her. Zanza, with blinding speed, raised her arm with the dagger and caught Boris in midair. The knife penetrated at the base of his throat and stuck out the back of his neck. There was no scream, only a loud thud as his body hit the ground. Orloff, in less than a heartbeat, was out of the door. Before Zanza could react, he reached out and grabbed her by the head with one arm, putting the other around her waist, and with his knee against her back applied all the strength he had, snapping her neck and back simultaneously. Orloff then fell at the side of his now-dead brother and cried like a baby.

After what seemed like hours, Orloff lifted himself up and went to the body of Zanza, which he then dragged into the house. As he looked around the room for something with which to start a fire, he could not help but notice the grinning skull on the shelf. He saw that it had a crack that very nearly split it in half. He wondered who the unfortunate soul was. Had Orloff been aware that it was Kavik, it is certain he would not have felt any sympathy. Zanza had grown tired of Kavik's constant complaining of his bodily ills due to his advanced age. Therefore, she reasoned that she would do them both a service by plunging the axe into the head of the sleeping and unsuspecting teacher of evil. Zanza was then fifteen years of age.

Orloff, finding nothing to burn, went outside and gathered some brush and returned to start the fire. Having removed the knife from the throat of Boris, he lifted his body and began the journey home.

The fire raged for three days and three nights, after which the land was purged.

CHAPTER 5

DRACULA'S REVENGE

The sun is down, and with the disappearance of its brilliance from the heavens, a night of horror and terror was about to begin and will continue for centuries to come. Dracula removed the lid from his box that had shielded him from the light of day. He then slowly stepped out, fully aware of his newly acquired strength and powers and knowing that before the night was over, these powers would have been tested to the utmost. Suddenly, without warning, an overpowering and maddening urge shook his being—he must have human blood! With arms outstretched, he willed a transformation of his body. Instantly, a strange and startling metamorphosis took place. In the place moments ago where Dracula stood, there now hovered a large gray bat two feet in length with spanned wings reaching four feet in width. Easily and silently, the bat flew out of the forest and stopped at the outskirts of the village where it encountered its first victim. The man was on his way to the inn for drink and talk as was his custom after a long day in the fields. As the bat swooped down, the man saw its shadow before him and turned to see what his eyes could not believe. The wings on the bat folded, and in its place stood a man. Paralyzed with fright, the man watched the outstretched hand take hold of him by the throat, lifting him several inches off the ground. Mercifully, his heart stopped as Dracula bit and tore out his throat, drinking his fill. His thirst quenched, he set out for his father's castle.

Val had just been placed in his bed by his servants, the merriment of the celebration having taken its toll on all who attended. He had barely closed his eyes when he felt a viselike grip on his ankle. He opened his eyes and saw his son leering before his face. He felt his ankle being crushed and heard the sound of bone breaking as he was being dragged out of the room. The shock and pain caused him to faint. When he awakened, he found himself shackled and hanging by his wrists in his own torture chamber. He then realized he was naked. He tried to speak but found he could not. He soon became aware that his tongue had been removed. For the first time it became apparent to him that he had been deceived. There was no bargain! As though reading his thoughts, Dracula reminded him of the master's promise that he would have life through his own son, for soon, Val's blood would run through the veins of his son. In mute silence, Val watched as Dracula placed before him several knives and selected the finest honed. Expertly, starting at the waist, he began to filet his father. Val was soon unconscious. This was not to be the end. Dracula then poured a mixture down his throat that would cause him to sleep until he returned the next evening.

Dracula then went in search of Lispeth. He found her alone in the guest chambers. He stripped and placed himself beside her. She awakened and saw his face reflected by the moonlight. Before she could say a word, he penetrated her with such force that her brain became numb, but she responded almost as fiercely. When he was finished with her, he told her he would be back the following evening. She reasoned that a great hoax had been played and was relieved to find that it was such. She had so many questions to ask; tomorrow she would get the answers when he returned. Dracula returned to his place of slumber with great expectations for the following night. Never had he felt so alive!

The body of the unfortunate victim, the first of Dracula's, was discovered at dawn. When examined by the local authority, the cause of death was attributed to wild animals. A closer inspection by a physician revealed the lack of blood in the corpse. The doctor, however, kept his findings to himself. The mayor ordered an intense search to begin. By sundown, tired and exhausted, the men returned to their homes.

The servants shouted the alarm to the guards in the castle at the discovery of the empty bedchambers of their master. All searched in vain. By late afternoon, the king ordered to make ready to depart after first light of the following day. Lady Lispeth, when told of her uncle's decision to leave, became apprehensive and asked of the king if she might delay her departure. With a clear mind for the first time in days since their arrival, the king felt the evil around him. Her request was denied.

The door to the barn flapped noisily back and forth as the wind increased in velocity. The mother sent her eldest daughter out to secure the door, and he was waiting. A short time later, the mother knelt beside her mutilated daughter in total shock. Once again, the local authority viewed the grizzly find, seeing the look of horror on the victim's lifeless face; he now realized that this was not the work of some wild animal. Alone with the doctor, he asked of his findings. The doctor informed him that the cause of death was the same as the first victim with one exception. He stated that the girl had been savagely violated. A later examination would reveal that the uterus had been crushed during the attack. When he informed the constable, they all wondered in God's name what kind of madman was capable of such a deed.

Dracula returned to the castle. All were astounded at his appearance, except for Lispeth, who was patiently waiting for the hour to be alone with him. As Dracula seated himself at the head of the table where the guests were having their evening meal, the king inquired as to the whereabouts of his father. Dracula feigned surprise and mild shock. He offered by way of explanation that his father undoubtedly had been called away on an urgent matter. As the servant poured a cup of wine before Dracula, it was instantly slapped aside. The poor servant was seized by the throat and thrown several feet from the table. Dracula quickly overcame his rage, because he did not want any show of violence before the king. He offered his apology to the guests, turned to the servant, still on the floor, and ordered that he was never to be served wine again. The king informed Dracula of his decision to depart at first light. Dracula suggested that all retire in order that they would be well rested for their long journey home. He then announced that he would be unable to see them off, as he must prepare to leave on a matter of importance this very night. The king was relieved, as he could not bear to look at that face again. He could not explain his own feelings of being terrified in the presence of this man. Dracula charmingly bid all farewells and departed.

Val opened his eyes as he felt the bites of the rodents on the lower part of his now—festering body. He attempted to shake and twist his body but was unable to do so. The pain was unbearable. He soon realized that he was being eaten alive. Suddenly, as the rodents leaped from his body, standing before him was Dracula, roaring with delight. He then picked up the knife and said softly to Val, "It is now time for me to finish the work." He then methodically stripped the remaining skin from Val's body. Just as Dracula completed his work, Val's body violently began to convulse. His eyes left their sockets.

CHAPTER 6

THE BAT

As Lispeth lay naked and waiting, Dracula entered the bedchambers. As he mounted her more violently than the first time, within a few minutes, she fainted. He wanted to tear at the warm flesh and drink his full, but he knew that the king would destroy the castle in vengeance. He could not afford to have the king and his mighty army as adversaries. Feeling quite pleased with himself after watching Val draw his last breath of life and seeing the rodents feasting on the body, he again turned his attention to Lispeth. She opened her eyes, and once again he took her, but not as fiercely. Even so, it would be necessary for her handmaiden to lift her out of bed and carry her the entire journey homeward. Lispeth would never know a man again in the physical sense, for he had nearly destroyed her womb.

The following morning, as Dracula slept the sleep of the dead, the people gathered at the graveside to mourn the dead. Afterwards, they looked to the man Orloff, for they knew of the courage he had shown, and they realized that a madman was in their midst. Orloff could only suggest they all bolt their doors and not venture from their homes after dark. When Orloff arrived home, he was surprised to find Paul, the monk, who had come to offer prayers for his dead brother and the other two victims. Paul attempted to explain why he could not give his blessing when Orloff, and his now-dead brother, came to him before the tragic journey. Orloff quickly interrupted and said it was he who should ask forgiveness. The two men agreed to let the matter drop. After supper, Orloff and his family gathered around Paul for prayer and to receive his blessing. As they did so, the evil approached at first in the form of a bat, and then in its place, Dracula stood! Now he would avenge the death of Zanza.

Orloff would be the last to die, but not until he had seen his loved ones slaughtered like cattle. And lastly, Orloff would satisfy Dracula's maniacal thirst.

As he approached, instantly, he was taken aback by the appearance of a blinding light, not unlike a halo, that surrounded the small farmhouse. It emanated a force of such purity that Dracula quaked in his own black soul, and he fled, cursing the heavens and those within.

Dracula was wild with rage as he came upon the next farmhouse. Although the door was bolted, with little effort, he tore the door from its hinges, and he mercilessly reaped his vengeance on a husband and wife and their four small children. The youngest, four years of age, he saved for last. Quenching his thirst while savoring each drop to the fullest, he then tossed the lifeless child into the fireplace and departed. Dracula's anger subsided after the brutal onslaught. He now reasoned that he must not lose such control of himself again. He knew fully well that a search would begin at daylight, and that he was most vulnerable at that time, should he be found. He quickly put the thought aside for the fools would never suspect him, nor for that matter come searching.

The burial was over the same morning they were found. Once again, the people turned to Orloff, who suggested that a search begin. While the search was on, Paul visited the homes of the men and blessed each one. The men searched in vain for five long days. The one redeeming factor was that no new victims were claimed. Dracula did attempt to enter several of the homes but was driven back by the same force that he encountered at Orloff's house. So in order to satisfy his craving for blood, he selected two of his many servants. Dracula, after his resurrection, now possessed far superior psychic powers and therefore knew that Paul was responsible for the temporary protection that people were now afforded.

CHAPTER 7

FRANCIS

Dracula devised a plan to destroy the holy man, and to do so, he would simply invite him to the castle. However, before he could do that, he needed more time for his powers to grow stronger. Then, and only then, could he confront and destroy the one mortal who posed a threat to his very being.

The disappearance of Val spread throughout the land. Never had the people had so much to be thankful for. There had been no new victims for the past six months, so they were confident that they had driven off the attacker and began to work their lands and prosper.

Val's army deserted soon after his disappearance, but Dracula did convince about a hundred to stay and serve him with the promise of double pay. During the six months that he did not venture out of the castle, twenty of the soldiers vanished. They met the same fate as the two servants before them.

Dracula was now ready to send for Paul. It was now time for the kill. That very evening he dispatched a servant with a handwritten invitation to Paul at the monastery. The trip took the messenger four days to return with Paul's refusal. Dracula's rage upon hearing that Paul had declined his invitation sent him on a murderous rampage. The first victim was his messenger. Once again, Dracula returned to the house of Orloff and, once more, he was unable to enter, because the force was even stronger than before. Orloff and his family were praying at the moment Dracula approached the house. This and the fact that Paul had implanted his cross on the outside of the door saved their lives. The next family was not as fortunate. He crashed through the door like a mad bull, taking the occupants totally by surprise. They attempted to defend themselves but were no match for this devil's own. Within the hour, he had finished his grizzly task, as usual, saving the eldest daughter for last. Tearing her clothing off her body, he sexually gratified himself to the fullest and then drank from her the lifesaving blood. The young girl of eighteen remained in shock after seeing the last member of her family torn apart. The nine unfortunate victims would not be found until noon the following day. Neither the doctor nor the constable, along with Orloff, could believe their eyes. The sight of the mangled bodies was beyond belief. Orloff wondered what kind of thing could tear the arms out of the sockets of the five very strong young sons of Vaslick. No one could give an answer. After the bodies were placed in hastily dug graves, Orloff asked the constable to send word to all the people to leave their homes and stay together in the village. Orloff left at once to seek out Paul, and on the road, he met a stranger; in fact, a monk, who was making his way to the monastery. Orloff was pleased to have the company of the young monk, making the journey much easier. He told him of the misfortunes that had befallen Transylvania for these many years and of the tyrannical rule of Val, whom he now believed to be among the dead. The young man listened intently as Orloff continued to reveal the tragic events of the past several months. Orloff said, "We are at a loss. There is no safety even in our homes. It is as though the devil himself is on the loose." The monk, saddened by the story, said, "Then, why are you going to the monastery, may I ask?" Orloff replied that he believed that Paul, the holy man, could help bring an end to the horror that had struck. How, he did not know, but when the good monk last visited their homes, there had not been a recurrence of the mass slaughtering for at least six months. "Now," said Orloff, "the demon is loose among us again." When they arrived at the monastery, they were informed that Paul could be found in the chapel. They entered and saw Paul in deep meditation. They joined him, and for several hours, the three men prayed. Afterwards, as evening fell, they shared a simple meal, and the young monk introduced himself as Francis to Paul. His mission was to visit and seek out the good brothers of the order and ask for their blessing, because he was new in the brotherhood and felt unworthy. Paul led the two men to his cell and, as they were seated, announced that he was about to reveal something that he had told only once; since he joined the holy order many years ago, the only person who knew about this was his confessor. When he had finished, he said to Francis, "My son, do you still feel that you are not worthy? What has happened to bring you here?" Orloff told of the need of the people for Paul to return and save them, for surely Satan was in their midst.

Francis spoke, "As I travel this land, there comes upon me the presence of evil, and I do believe Orloff is right, that Satan is among us—Lucifer, the morning star, the most beautiful of heavenly inhabitants. During the impending rebellion of Lucifer, the Lord knew what was in the heart of Lucifer, and he confronted him, saying, 'Why hast thou allowed envy to enter your heart?' Lucifer answered, 'Why should not all who are here bow and worship me? Am I not the most radiant of all?' Hearing this, the Lord saddened and said, 'Satan, leave my sight.' And so Satan gathered his legions, and they were many, and a great first war began. God called upon Michael, his archangel, to champion his cause, so Michael then gathered his army of angels to fight. The heavens opened as the battle raged, and Satan, with his followers, were cast out. As they fell, they cursed the Lord. The Lord replied, 'You will never look at my face again, and you will live in your hell which you have created.' As they fell, their appearance was changed, and they grew horns and tails for all time. Satan swore vengeance as the stars shook in the heavens.

"So, my friends, I fear this is his work, for he has great power. But do not despair for we have the protection of the Lord." Francis continued, "The Lord knew that he aspired for the throne and, therefore, became an adversary, so his name was changed from Lucifer, meaning light, to Satan, meaning darkness. The Almighty gave him his own kingdom the dark world, and he then became the Prince of Darkness. Satan swore to have revenge against all that was opposite himself. So he was determined to torment and tempt mankind and vie for the souls of men that truly belong to God." Orloff asked, "What can we do against one so powerful?" Francis answered, "God created all things, but he gave man as well as the angels free will to think and choose as he wished. But if man needs help, all that is required is to ask, and through our prayers, the Lord will give his protection. Come now, let us pray, and tomorrow we will meet the challenge."

Paul showed the two men to their cells. He then announced that at first light, there was someone he would like them to meet. "So good night, my friends, and may God be with us." Orloff fell into a deep sleep because he was totally exhausted. Not so though with Francis and Paul, for they were in their rooms quietly praying to God for guidance and help in the long struggle that they knew lay ahead of them.

CHAPTER 8

THE CHALLENGE

Early the next morning after a breakfast of goat's milk and bread, Paul led them to a small room. There, looking very pale but a little stronger than she was five weeks ago when first brought by her uncle's soldiers, was Lispeth. She sat up as the three men approached her bedside. Paul presented Francis and Orloff and then asked if she would please repeat what she had told him when she first arrived at the monastery. First, Paul explained how Lispeth was near death when she was first taken there, but with the help of the brothers of the monastery, who kept a constant bedside vigil as they prayed for her immortal soul, God answered their prayers, and Lispeth began to regain her strength.

Paul took Lispeth's hand, "It is most important that you tell all just as you told me, so that we may help." Lady Lispeth began her story. "The king, my uncle, summoned me to tell me it was time for me to take a husband and prepare immediately for a journey that very morning. I asked where we were going, and he replied to the castle of Val. There I would meet Val's son, Count Dracula, my husband-to-be. All went well on the journey that took several days, and to be truthful, I was filled with excitement and anticipation with the thought of meeting my betrothed. I prayed that he would be handsome, or at least pleasant to look at, and I also wondered and hoped he would find me beautiful. My handmaidens teased me, saying I would grow fat bearing many children. I laughed with them, saying it mattered not if that be the wish of my husband, but that they would have to care for them—all fourteen of them. How we laughed at such a thought. We could hardly wait for morning to come. The king had said that this was the last night of the journey and that before noon they would enter the castle." As she reflected on the past with tears falling from her eyes, she continued, "That night was the last time I heard the sound of laughter from my lips. What a fool I must be." Francis dried her eyes and reassured her that any young woman that was about to enter into the holy state of matrimony would feel and act the same. She found his words reassuring, but it was the sound of his voice, the tone of which sounded like a strange, beautiful instrument, along with his eyes, which was the clearest gray that she had ever seen. She felt as though his eyes were absorbing all of her pain. She continued with a sense of well-being that now had taken hold of her.

"Although the sun was very bright and the day clear, a little before noon, as the king had promised, the journey had come to an end. As we halted momentarily, there stood the castle, and a feeling of foreboding came over me. It seemed so strange that the sun, though directly overhead, should cast such an eerie shadow over the giant structure that lay before us. The king's captain gave the order to step up the pace for the king was anxious to enter the castle and rid himself of the dust of travel and avail himself of the hospitality of his host. At first meeting, I found Val to be very gracious and somewhat overjoyed at our arrival, but I felt it was not his nature to act so. The other guests had arrived, and all were presented to the king as they entered the huge dining room for the noon meal. Val announced that after the ladies had eaten and rested, I would meet his son at the evening meal. I was most grateful and relieved, as I wanted to look my very best upon meeting my husband-to-be. I felt somewhat ashamed of my ill thoughts of Val and promised myself not to allow such things to enter my head again." At that time, she had not known of the reputation of the murderer, Val the Impaler. The women of the king's court were not allowed to be present when such matters were discussed. It was only after she had left the castle, three days later, when the captain, who had been in charge of the escort, told her about the madman. He did so because he thought it would help her in some way. It did explain the foreboding feeling that had come over her when she first saw the castle, as well as the almost instant dislike toward Val. Lispeth continued, "I fell into a deep sleep and was surprised when awakened and informed that it was near time to join the other guests and to meet the young count. As I entered the room, he, the count, was seated. Val escorted me to his son's side, and without a word he turned and left. From that very moment, when he took my hand and looked into my eyes, I had no will of my own. It was as though I lived in a dreamworld of shadows. I was aware of the merrymaking all around me, but I became less aware after the count returned from the dead." Seeing the startled faces before her, Lispeth quickly explained how the count suddenly fell from the table as though dead. "And at that very moment, I felt I had received my soul. Val announced to the startled guest that his son was now with the dead. I was taken aback when he then ordered that the feast continue." She then remembered that she fainted. Lispeth then told of the reappearance of Dracula and the disappearance of Val the following day. "Upon seeing the count enter and telling that his death was all in play for the amusement of the guests, he then seated himself by my side, and I was compelled to look directly into his eyes, and when I did so, I saw death. Once again, I had no will or control of my actions." She then told of how he would come to her in the night and do with her as he wishes. The one thing she now remembered was the strong feeling that he wanted to kill her. Then, when her uncle, the king, was informed of her illness, he ordered that she be made ready to leave the castle at once. She recalled having resisted his command, but why, she did not know. After returning home in deathlike state and lying in what all thought was her deathbed, she related how she could hear Dracula calling to her to return to him. After several attempts of trying and being prevented by the king's guards or her handmaidens, the king became fearful that a curse had befallen her. After all, he had the best physicians who were at a loss to explain or find a cure for her strange illness. The king grieved for his niece and felt that he was the cause

THE ALPHA DRACULA · 49

of her suffering, because if he had not taken her to Val's, this curse would not have befallen her. He now admitted that he himself had sensed some sort of evil at the castle. So therefore, he decided to send Lispeth to the monastery for safety, in the hope that it would save her life. "Now you must rest," said Paul. "It is good the king sent you to us, for the shadow of death indeed has passed from you, and you are growing stronger. But I fear you must remain with us until we can be sure of your safety."

"Do not worry," said Francis, "for God will be with you." The three men then left as peace came over Lispeth that she had not known before. Paul led the two men to the chapel, saying it was time for the noon prayer, after which they would partake of the noon meal. Orloff asked, "May it not be something of more substance than breakfast?" Paul smiled and answered, "Yes," much to Orloff's relief.

True to his word, after prayer, they ate mutton, cheese, and figs. To quench their thirst, and to Orloff's delight, a large pitcher of goat's milk with baked bread was served. As they again sat in Paul's small cell, Orloff was the first to speak.

"Can a man return from the dead? What matter of creature must we deal with?" Paul answered, "If it be so, then it must be the work of Satan, for he is truly powerful."

"Yes," said Francis, "but not all-powerful. Now it seems that all of this new treachery that plagues the people of your village, Orloff, began at the time of Lady Lispeth's visit to the castle."

Paul and Orloff quickly agreed. Paul then told of the messenger who came to him with a request of Count Dracula to visit the castle and of his refusal to do so.

"Perhaps, it is a good thing you declined, for I fear your life would have been taken," said Francis.

"Why do you think my life would have been taken? After all, I am old and could be of no threat to Dracula," Paul said.

Francis asked Paul, "Is it not true, according to Orloff on our journey here to the monastery, that after your visit to the homes and village of the people, the killings ceased for about six months' time?"

"Well, even so," replied Paul, "I don't understand what my visit had to do with the temporary halt of these monstrous murders. I did think that my prayers had been answered by our Lord for the safe protection of our people, but now after hearing from our good friend,

Orloff, of the recurrence of the foul deeds, I am at a loss to understand what you are implying." Francis looked into Paul's eyes and saw the pain and confusion, but with an inner strength of faith that he had not seen in any man. "Dear brother Paul, I do believe that God did indeed answer your prayers, and I do believe that your presence was felt by the evil one. And therefore, he was repelled from further attacks until now. I can only guess that he has grown stronger, and I also think that is why you were asked to visit the castle. I am certain that you would have met death before your arrival." Orloff wondered how in God's name one so young knew so much. As though reading his mind, Francis said, "I have taken into account all that has been said by the two of you, and after hearing Lady Lispeth recount her tragic experience, I am convinced that the cause and solution lies within the castle."

"How can we fight such a thing?" Orloff pleaded.

"With the sword of the Lord," Francis replied.

"Then we must prepare to leave to face this demon, and may God be with us," said Paul.

"No, good brother, I will go alone, and with your blessing, may I be worthy to meet the challenge."

"I will go with you," said Orloff.

"Thank you, good sir, but I fear that we will be at the very gates of hell, and I may not be worthy to do God's work."

But Orloff insisted, "You will need me to guide you as you are a stranger in this land. I also want to help bring an end to this evil that has befallen this land of ours."

Dracula indeed had been growing stronger and more aware of his powers but was still annoyed that Paul had refused his invitation. Of course, his plan was as Francis had guessed that Paul would have been met by two of his soldiers and quickly dispatched halfway to his destination. Now, Dracula formulated a new scheme which was quite simple—he would send two soldiers to the monastery to take Paul's life. Their reward would be their death. He could not allow that someday drunk they would loosen their tongues and reveal that he had ordered the death of Paul. His fear was that it would unite the people of Transylvania, and they would storm the castle. He was well aware that he did not have enough men to defend such a siege.

Orloff and his family were also on his death list. The thought of sending assassins to do away with them had occurred to him, but he wanted to reserve that pleasure for himself. The cross on the door was the only thing that prevented him from doing so. It would only be a matter of time, he mused, after all, what is time? Had he not an eternity?

Dracula was becoming impatient with the confines of the castle. He longed for the gaiety of the European nights, but the time for such a trip was not yet at hand. He summoned several of his servants and gave them a list of guests that he wished would attend a feast that he was hosting. The reason, even though one was not needed, was to celebrate his birth. He roared with laughter at the thought, because in truth, had he not been born again? It was not as though those invited were in need of a reason. For them, any excuse would do. They were among the worst of the idle rich, indulging themselves with wine and pleasures of the flesh at any opportunity. They numbered fifty; he anticipated the festivities would last for several weeks. Of course, not quite as many would return, and that thought pleased and excited him.

CHAPTER 9

RING OF FIRE

The constable, with the aid of volunteers, organized the people as they came into the village from their farms for safety. They numbered about two hundred, plus a hundred that already lived in the village, making a total of three hundred in all. The constable's plan was somewhat ingenious. First, it was forbidden for anyone to leave the confines of the village; second, a ring of fire was maintained around the village beginning at sundown until sunup; third, the men would share in the work of their farms. Those that lived in about a sixty-mile radius were told to bring their stock and divide it among the nearby farms. They were divided into groups of twenty to complete this task. Once having done so, they could leave the safety of the village at sunup, attend the stock, and return within two hours of darkness. The men who remained were assigned the task of going to the nearby forest to cut down trees in order to maintain the nightly fires. Above all this, the constable was at a loss, being a realist; he knew that the present situation could not continue indefinitely. He also felt that there was an unnatural and evil force about. The first time he had labored to explain his thoughts to the physician, he was taken aback at how readily he agreed. They also agreed that they should not confide their thoughts with anyone else, for fear that the populace would panic and run amuck. However, they did suspect that their beliefs were shared by many.

"What of the holy one?" asked the constable. "Have you taken notice of the fact that after his last visit to our village, the attacks had ceased for about six months?"

"Yes," replied the doctor, "and he may be our only hope."

It flew from farm to farm in search of human prey, its wings beating noisily. It became more frantic with the realization that its prey had fled. Now, as this thing from hell circled the village, unable to penetrate the flames, it now took its human form and raised his fist and cursed all within the protection of the flame. Did they think that their feeble efforts would prevent him from fulfilling his needs? He then filled the night air with the sound of his laughter, thinking that they reminded him so much of cattle penned together. After all, there would be other nights. Once again, resuming the form of the bat and returning from whence he came, he saw below a small group of travelers camped about eight miles from the village. All were asleep, but one. The young man, about twenty, had just stepped out into the clearing, feeling much better now that he had relieved himself and thinking only of returning to a much-needed sleep. But his thoughts of sleep were instantly abandoned as he saw with horror his eldest brother, as though plucked from the ground with one hand and being lifted into the air, then tossed with such force striking head first at a nearby tree, causing it to crack open like an egg. Paralyzed with fright, he watched as this thing fell on his brother's wife, and in what seemed like an instant, she had been stripped and lay naked. Her screams brought him out of his shock; he ran to the attacker and fell upon him. As he did so, he found himself looking into the face of the evil one himself. His strength deserted him as he realized that there was no earth beneath his feet. As his body was hurled in the direction of his brother, he saw in the clear moonlight his own head in the same condition. He heard only the sound as his head began to crack. The other members of the group were quickly disposed of, except for the old woman who had awakened at the sound of the younger woman's scream. Her sick heart could not withstand what her eyes beheld. She fell back into the cart where she had been sleeping with the younger woman's infant child, her body now shielding the baby from Dracula's vicious attack. Dracula now turned his attention to the hysterical woman who now was in a kneeling position. He seized her by the hair and forced her to the ground on her back and then entered her. She pleaded with him to spare her life, and as she continued to plead, each thrust became more unbearable. Her pleas only excited him and drove him to higher sexual gratification. As she was about to beg that she had an infant to care for, he bit and tore out her jugular vein and did drink his fill as he reached climax.

The morning hours would bring discoveries of the unfortunate travelers. Out of seven, only the infant was saved by the body of the old woman. The group of men who came upon the unfortunate victims was horrified at their find. The bodies were hurriedly buried, and a moment was taken for a silent prayer for the poor souls. One of them returned to the village with the infant, and the others proceeded to tend to their chores and vowed to return to the village much sooner than the two hours allotted them before dark.

With each passing hour, Lady Lispeth grew stronger. As she sat outdoors in the morning sun, revealing her radiant face, she knew she had become a whole woman once again. How this happened, she did not know; she only knew that the healing process began the moment Francis had taken her hand. Never had she met a man so gentle and yet so strong.

Francis had left Paul and Orloff, saying that he was going to prepare himself with prayer and fasting at the small cave which lay about one hundred feet from the monastery. Orloff asked how long he would be gone. Francis answered that only God would decide and then asked Paul and Orloff to pray for him, and he departed.

"How can he gain strength by fasting?" asked Orloff.

"By fasting, his soul and mind will grow stronger, and through his prayer, his body will be fed; our God is willing, and I do believe this to be so. Although Francis does not yet realize that there was a purpose for his coming to Transylvania, it was to do with the work of the Lord our God. Come, let us and the other brothers join in prayer for him and give thanks," Paul replied.

As Lispeth sat lost in her thoughts, she suddenly became aware of Francis; his presence had such a calming effect as he took her hand in his and said how pleased he was with her much-improved appearance. She drew his hand to her lips and kissed the palm of his hand. Raising her head and looking into his eyes, she asked him to sit with her. He smiled and did so.

"What can I do for you, my child?" Francis asked.

To this, Lispeth replied, "I know that I should not say what I am about to say, but I feel I must. I love you, and I never want to leave you. I know that you have given your life to God and would never look at me as a woman the way men do, but all I ask is that you let me be near and serve you until death do us part. I know I am not worthy and beg that you consider what I have said." Francis gazed into her now-tearful eyes and, as his own eyes began to moisten, replied, "It is I who is not worthy of the love you have offered me, and I truly thank you. You are a young and very beautiful woman, and soon you will have the kind of love with a man that I am unable to give you. Please, Lady Lispeth, do not think I do not love you. I love you as I do all of God's creatures. When this horror that has stricken this land is brought to an end, you will return to your home and find the happiness that you so richly deserve. So be of good faith, my dear, dear Lispeth." He then knelt and kissed her foot. Rising slowly, he then left. And again, he left her with a peace that she knew would stay with her until the day she died.

After two weeks had passed, Francis emerged from his place of penance, looking none the worst from his ordeal. The one hundred seventy-five pounds that his five-foot eleven-inch frame once carried was now reduced to one hundred fifty pounds. Paul was the first to see him as he entered where all had just seated themselves after giving thanks for their noon meal. They were stunned at his appearance. Never had they seen anyone with such calm about himself. Truly a handsome figure of a man, he generated a strength absorbed by all present. After their meal, Francis announced that he would depart with Orloff; it was now time to go to the castle of Count Dracula and bring to an end, with the help of God, the evil force that has plagued the children of the Lord our God.

Paul asked Francis, "Might it not be better to wait until morning when you would be more rested?"

"I think not, brother Paul, for I feel the time is now to meet the challenge."

"We shall pray for you and Orloff until your return," Paul assured them.

The guests arrived at the castle of Dracula on the same day Francis and Orloff left the monastery. The servants had been instructed to attend to the needs of his guests and inform them that he would greet them at the evening meal. Shortly after sunset, Dracula entered the great hall where the festivities were in progress. "Welcome and good evening," he announced as he entered. "I trust your journey to Dracula Castle was a pleasant one." They answered in the affirmative. Some gathered around and inquired as to his whereabouts for the past year. He replied that it was not quite a year since he had seen most of them. Also, the business of his father's estates that had been thrust upon him so unexpectedly demanded his personal attention. He excused himself and beckoned a servant to fetch the two guards at the front entrance and bring them to him. When they appeared, he ordered them to go to the monastery and bring back the head of Paul. They were also to find the woman, Lady Lispeth, and return her unharmed. "Upon your return, you shall be greatly rewarded." With visions of wealth, they left immediately. Dracula rejoined his guests, noticing that several of the women were very beautiful, and he looked forward to bedding with them.

The two would-be assassins came upon the sleeping form of Orloff. They did not see Francis who was about ten feet off to the side of the sleeping Orloff. He had just completed his nightly prayer, and as the two men with swords raised were about to strike their mark, they heard the sound of Francis's voice, asking, "Why would you do murder?" They were stunned, for they were sure the man they were about to kill was alone. Orloff leaped to his feet and took them by surprise, for they momentarily took their eyes from him to follow the sound of Francis's voice. Orloff sent a smashing blow to the face of the larger of the two, causing him to fall to his knees and drop his sword to the ground. Orloff then took hold of the other by his arm, twisting it with such force that the arm broke at the wrist and elbow. He then threw the now-screaming man on top of the other and picked up a sword with the thought of slaying the cowering men. Francis stepped by his side and calmly asked, "Would you blacken your soul with their blood on your hands?"

Orloff replied, "I already have the blood of one on my hands, may God forgive me."

"Ask, and it shall be so," answered Francis. He then prepared to administer aid to the injured man. He then asked the men, "Why are you about the devil's work?"

The larger one spoke, "Never have I received mercy such as you have shown. We do deserve to die, and we thank you for our lives." They were in shock; never before had they thanked anyone. Francis talked to the men for hours, telling of the goodness and love of God. After which, they all slept. At daybreak, they again thanked Francis and said that they would not return to their master and promised never to raise arms against another man.

"This will be the last night of our journey, because we will arrive at the castle at sundown," said Orloff.

"I am sorry, my friend, I'll go alone; you must see to your family," replied Francis. Orloff protested vigorously. "I cannot allow you to face whatever it is alone."

"My friend, you have forgotten; I will not be alone. Do I not take with me the prayers of all at the monastery?"

"And mine also," Orloff replied. The night was exceptionally warm for that time of year. Orloff tried to stay awake and keep watch as Francis prayed, but his efforts were in vain. As the warm air gently blew over him, he began to hear, ever so softly, the sound of humming. He closed his eyes and listened to the lullaby that his mother had always hummed whenever as a child he was troubled and could not sleep. As Francis approached the sleeping Orloff, there came about a bitter cold. He bent and picked up the discarded cloak and laid it over his sleeping and smiling companion. He attempted to gather some loose branches to build a fire but found the wood was nearly frozen. Suddenly, he looked up and saw a shadow of a man. As the figure came closer, Francis pulled his cloak tighter about himself. The cold was unbearable. He was unable to see the face because the moon had disappeared behind the clouds. He could see that he was formidable, well over six feet, about 6 feet 4 inches, and easily two hundred forty pounds. The stranger spoke as he approached within eight feet of Francis.

"Greetings, fellow traveler, may I join you and your companion?"

"Why do you attempt to deceive me, O' Fallen Star? Do you think that our Creator would not make you known to me? For your darkness fills the very night," Francis answered.

And with a voice that shook the very ground, the dark angel answered, "Do you think that you can undo my work and destroy he who pays homage to me?"

Before Francis could reply, he continued in a much-calmer manner, "If you will kneel before me, I will raise you above all men. I will give you power over him that you seek, and men will glorify you as no man ever before."

Francis fell to his knees, and with his crucifix outstretched, he looked to the heavens and cried aloud, "My God, my God, shed your light about this place so that this evil one may be cast into the darkness of whence he came." Instantly, the clouds departed, and the moon shone with a brilliance never before seen by man. The moonbeams fell upon Francis so that he thought he was in the light of the morning sun. He continued to pray as a rush of cold air passed over him, and with the sound of thunder, his cry for help was answered. "Why is my cloak about me on a warm night such as this?" asked Orloff, rubbing his heavy-laden eyes. "I am sorry, my friend, I thought you might have been a little cold. Please return to your sleep, for the light of day will be upon us very soon."

"Is it not strange that we grow so few in number with each passing night?" asked the corporal to the men around him.

"Captain, I tell you, we must leave this place. Our comrades are disappearing, and he that we serve tells us they are deserters."

"What do you think happened to them?" asked the captain.

"I do not know, but some were my good friends, and I know they would not have left, at least not without asking me to join them. Also, I tell you that in all the battles I have fought, I have feared no man, have known no fear until I first saw him!"

"I too wonder at the disappearance of our comrades," replied the captain, not wanting to admit that he too felt fear at the sight of his employer.

"Yes, we are soldiers, not guards. Tell the other men we will leave this place in the morning." No one noticed the burning red eyes of the bat overhead on a ledge of the castle wall with its mouth half open, exposing razor-sharp teeth.

The attack began approximately a half hour after the men fled the castle. The corporal was the first the larger of the bats claimed. Before any of the men could react, hundreds of bats fell upon them. Their screams and cries of pain were soon replaced by the slurping sounds of the now-bloated bats as they drank of the thick red substance of their prey.

The naked woman stood before him. He watched as she abandoned all modesty as she now moved about the room. She helped herself to more wine, asking, "What do you think my husband would do if he found us together, my dear Count?"

"Slut, what do I care for the feeling of that fool or any of you? All of you are here for my pleasure." The tone of his voice caused her to panic as she reached for her clothes. He sprang upon her like a wild animal and violently took her. When he had finished with her, he ordered her to return to her husband until he had further need of her.

Late the next day, Francis and Orloff came upon the bodies of the soldiers. "They are from the castle," said Orloff. "What kind of animal could do this to so many? Look at this one," he said, pointing to the corporal, "his arms have been torn out. Do you see that their throats have been eaten away? It is the same as the others that I have told you about. So many men, and they could not defend themselves. Please, I beg of you, do not go to the castle."

"Let us pray for these unfortunate ones," said Francis. "It will soon be dark, so you must hurry." After Francis had finished, he turned to Orloff, "Now you must leave and go to the village. I can find my way from here. Thank you, my friend, and may God be with you."

"May he be with you, Holy One," Orloff answered.

Francis arrived at the castle and was admitted by a servant. The servant, thinking he was a late arrival, led him to where other guests were assembled for the evening meal. Francis asked to be presented to his master. Dracula was in the treasury room, taking inventory of the wealth that Val had plundered. He knew that he must leave at least for a while, and it would be necessary to purchase property in other lands. Of course, he would never have to concern himself with the need for riches; it would be his for the taking. His thoughts were interrupted as a servant announced that a visitor wished to see him. "Someone from the village?" asked Dracula.

"I do not believe so; his dress is of another land."

"Bring him to me." As the servant took his leave, a feeling of apprehension came about Count Dracula. While the servant left to inform his master of the visitor, Francis announced to all, in a loud voice that caused some to drop their cups of wine in astonishment, to leave this place if they feared for their life and mortal souls. He picked up one of the many candelabras and tossed it at the heavily draped window. All stood their ground, until Francis shouted again in a voice that caused their spines to grow weak. Those who were standing had to reach for tables and chairs for support. The drapes slowly began to flame; there was panic as they all fled. Francis saw the servant appear. "Take me to him, and then you leave this place." Francis was led down a deep and winding corridor that was only lit by a few candles every twenty feet or so. "In here, sir," the servant said in a voice that was barely audible. He then fled, for he knew that his life depended on the speed that his legs could muster. Francis entered the room; Dracula, without turning, asked, "Why have you come?"

"To put an end to your reign of terror."

"Fool, you have come to die. Do you think that you can defeat me? I, who have found favor in the eyes of the Prince of Darkness?"

"I beg of you, denounce the devil and ask our God for his mercy so that you may regain your soul."

Dracula slowly turned to face Francis. Francis fell back as he saw the face of a man changed into that of a bat bearing razor-sharp teeth and eyes that glowed with the fires from hell. He advanced toward Francis. Quickly regaining his composure, Francis put his hand to his side, removed his cross, and held it to his heart. Dracula fell back as though struck by a bolt of lightning. The scream that came from his throat shook the foundation of the castle. His face transformed to its human form as he fell to the floor as though one dead. Francis turned and slowly left the room, closing the door and removing the padlock, and then placing his cross in its place. "This will be your tomb. No more shall you seek human prey." Francis emerged from the smoke-filled castle just as several of the last guests to leave were driving off, luggage free, in their carriages. He slowly made his way in the direction of the village. The following day, he arrived and was quite pleased to see Paul and Orloff.

Orloff, with tears streaming down his face, said, "I had feared for your safety and thought I would never see you again."

"You should have more faith, my friend."

"Tell us what happened, did you see him whom you sought?" asked Orloff.

Francis replied, "Give the news to the people that they may return to their homes."

"That is indeed good to hear, for I did not think the people could continue to live much longer under the present conditions," said Paul. The constable explained to Francis how they kept the village surrounded by fire at night, and in doing so, they kept the monster from further attacks. "It was not the fire alone that saved you from harm, but the collective prayers of all of you. Continue to do so, and you will have the protection of the Lord."

After two days of rest, Francis announced that he must return to his own land. The people of the village thanked him and gave him provisions for the long journey home. He was given a mule to carry the burden, which he refused.

"Good-bye, my son," said Paul.

There were many to wish Francis a fond farewell. They watched until he was out of sight. Orloff turned to Paul and asked, "Why did he come?"

"Let it be enough that he did come, and we should all give thanks to Francis of Assisi," Paul answered.

Footnote

Saint Francis of Assisi was the Little Flower, the man who could speak to the animals as well as the birds; the strange phenomenon that they obeyed and loved him amazed everyone. Saint Francis of Assisi (1182-1228) founded the San Franciscans' Order. He was born to a wealthy family. His father was Pietro Bernardone, and his mother, the daughter of a wealthy merchant. Francis had dreams and visions. One of the 'first happened when he was about twenty-two or twenty-four years of age. As he knelt in the little chapel, San Damaino, in prayer before the cross, the eyes of Jesus, as well as the mouth, opened and said, "Francis, repair my house, as you can see it is in ruin." The statement was repeated three times. Francis, thinking that he was told to actually repair the chapel as it was in bad need of repair, left and returned the same day with all the money he had and gave it to the priest. But the priest would not accept the money. So he asked if he could stay and begin his training for the cleric and, while there, repair the wall, floors, and the roof. He also went to other nearby churches and did the same. He gave away all he owned and took the oath of poverty. He soon gathered a number of disciples. He then went to Pope Innocent III and was given permission to form his own order—the Poor Men of Christ. Francis traveled the countryside, giving comfort to the sick and poor. His sermons inspired all. It is a matter of record that he had been seen often levitating as high as twenty feet and, sometimes, much higher. From the time he began his cleric training, he had prayed to God to be allowed to share the suffering of Jesus Christ. His prayers were answered when Jesus appeared and spoke to him. What was said, Francis did not reveal. But as he lay on the cold floor, the stigma appeared. His hands and feet began to bleed, as well as his side. This would occur until he died. This was also attested to by at least a hundred witnesses including Pope Alexander IV. After four years of illness and suffering, the Little Flower died. In his lifetime he was thought to be a saint. Two years after his death in 1228, he was canonized.

CHAPTER 10

THE FORBIDDEN ROOM

Eighty years had passed, and during that time, Transylvania enjoyed peace and prosperity. But the people remained superstitious with the retelling of the carnage from generation to generation. None would dare set foot on the estate of Dracula's castle. Now, with the passing years, the people ceased to heed the advice that Francis had given. After all, time had expired all who survived the carnage. Most were beginning to think the stories were old wives' tales or, the very least, overly exaggerated. Such were the thoughts of the two foolish young men, thieves, in fact—Bolac and Karva, who were just released from confinement, as so often was the case. They were suspected of murder, but it could not be proven. Now they reasoned that the castle contained vast treasure that could be theirs for the taking. Bolac, the leader of the two, assured Karva that there was nothing to fear.

"Had not the castle been deserted these many years, and thanks to fear and superstition, none have dared to enter," Bolac said.

Karva readily agreed, "Yes, and with our wealth, we can leave this place and live like kings. When shall we start to collect our fortune?"

"Early tomorrow, after we steal a mule and cart each to carry out our plunder."

"We will not get there until dark," said Karva, trying to keep the sound of panic out of his voice.

But it did not escape Bolac. "Fool, do you want to travel all night? We will need the light of day to make our way about the castle and locate the treasure. Now, let us sleep, for it will be several days before we can close our eyes again." At sundown, they were five hundred feet from the castle. The castle loomed ominously in its barren surroundings; the sight of which would have caused any God-fearing man to turn on his heels in fright. "It is freezing cold here. How can this be," said Kava, "when only a moment ago it was very warm?"

"We will warm ourselves when we get inside."

"Hurry," answered Bolac. They pulled at their mules, but they resisted. Bolac began to shout and beat the one he had been leading. His efforts were in vain.

"Look at the way they choke," cried Karva as the mules broke free of their carts and ran back in the direction they had come. Karva broke out in a sweat. He visibly shook from head to toe as he took hold of Bolac and said, "Look at the castle. I can barely see it. There is so much dust blowing, and yet there is not a sound of wind." Bolac felt a viselike grip take hold of his limbs, but the hold was from within. He could not explain this strange sensation. If he could, he would have recognized fear. He fought to regain his composure, and after a few minutes, he succeeded. He took hold of Karva with his right hand on his throat, and with his left holding a knife to his stomach, he gritted, "If you do not stop acting like a woman, I will kill you. Now, let us take hold of the carts and do what we came to do." They entered the castle, finding the door partly open. Karva couldn't keep from asking himself over and over, "How can the wind blow without sound, and why was it freezing cold when inside the castle was warm?" There was no fire in the fireplace. He should have run with the mules. Instead he allowed himself to be forced to take the first step on the threshold of hell. His thoughts of doom were interrupted by Bolac shouting, "Quick, find candles, so we can light our way." Two minutes later, Karva had located twenty candles. The light they gave off as he lit each one diminished his fear to a small degree. As they entered the large room where the guests had fled the fire eighty years before, they could see that it had contained itself in the room, since the castle had been built of stone, and even the floors were marble. The walls had been draped, and of course, they, along with the oak furniture, were destroyed by the fire. The gold and silver candelabras, somewhat twisted by the heat of the fire, piled by the door from which they entered. Karva said, "We have only to gather the goblets and plates of gold, and we will have enough to make us rich."

"No," answered Bolac, "we must find the treasury room. Come, it must be below." After searching about an hour, they came upon that which they sought.

"This is the last room; it must be here," said Bolac.

"How can it be? There is no lock, only a cross where the lock should be. See how it glows. Please, let us not enter," pleaded Karva.

His patience at an end with his cohort, Bolac replied, "It is only the light from the candles." He then slammed his fist into Karva's face, causing his nose to flatten evenly with his upper lip. The blood began to run freely down his mouth and chest. As Karva screamed in pain, Bolac lifted the cross out of the slot and tossed it ten feet down the dark corridor. He then pushed the heavy steel door open. The blow had caused Karva to drop the two candles he had been holding. "Now pick up the candles, coward," he ordered, "and light our way in." Karva did so, and they stepped inside.

Bolac shouted, "I knew it, I knew it," as he looked to the left where they were standing. He ran and fell on one of the several open chests that were filled with jewels and gold coins. "Put the candles down and help me." Karva did as he was told, putting one of the candles on top of the closed chest. He then turned to his right. He knew at once that he had walked into hell as he looked into the maniacal face of this nameless demon that had seized and held him in a viselike grip. Surely it must be from hell. The fiery black eyes burned into his brain. He could smell and feel the foul breath of this thing as it drew him within inches of its mouth. How strange, he thought, that he could smell. Had not the bones in his nose been broken and shattered? He opened his mouth to scream, but no sound came forth as Dracula bit into the side of Karva's throat and drank greedily. Bolac turned at the sound of breaking bones as Karva's body was slammed into the solid stone wall where it slid to the floor like a sawdust doll of a child. Instantly, he knew that all the gold was useless. Only one thing mattered, and that was his life. He bolted through the door and ran faster than he ever did before in his life. He listened for the sound of pursuing footsteps, but there were none, only the sound of laughter. As he made his way up from the dungeon corridor and breathlessly made his way to the door, he turned to look back and could not believe what he saw. It was the largest black dog he ever saw. It was some fifteen feet behind him. He heard the most terrifying scream filling his head. In a second, he realized that it was he who was responsible. His way to safety was barred by the candelabras that he and Karva had placed in front of the door. He tripped and crashed down on top of the booty, his body twisting. He was face up as the beast, with his front paws, pinned him down. This time he knew that he had met fear face-to-face for the first time in his life, as he saw the horror-stricken eyes, the transformation of beast to man, and listened as he spoke, who surely he thought must be Satan himself. "You, I will keep and savor." Dracula placed the unconscious body of Bolac side by side with the skeletal remains of Val, with the exception that he allowed his feet to touch the floor. He then placed a table by his side. On it he placed a gold goblet. Bolac began to moan as he slowly regained consciousness. "Come now, you have had enough sleep" and with that, he delivered a back hand to the left side of Bolac's face, causing the limp head to snap back and loosen several teeth. The blow was effective as Bolac's tearful eyes opened. Coughing and choking on his own blood, he spit out three teeth. His eyes cleared, focusing on the leering face before him.

"Welcome to Dracula's Castle, my greedy friend. You will, of course, remain as my guest."

Bolac's cunning brain began to function. His instinct for survival overcame his fear. If only this thing will leave me alone, maybe I can find a way to save myself, he thought. Dracula, seeing that his victim was alert, began to strip Bolac. After doing so, he took a knife and examined it.

"Yes, this will do. Don't you agree?" he said, holding it up for Bolac's inspection. He then bent down and lifted Bolac's genitals and placed the point of the knife on the vein an inch from the rectum. He then pushed ever so gently. Removing the knife, he had penetrated an eighth of an inch. Swiftly, before a drop of blood had poured out of the wound, he placed the gold goblet between Bolac's legs, and within minutes, his cup was full. Bolac had screamed and wished for the solace of unconsciousness, but he was not afforded that luxury. Dracula then took dirt from the floor and allowed some blood to mix with it and placed the now-muddy substance on the wound, thereby stopping the flow of blood.

Now standing, he raised the cup to Bolac and said, "Here's to my friend, and may my cup not run over. For you will be with me a long time." He then drank, as Bolac looked on in horror. It was almost dawn. Dracula excused himself but returned shortly with a cup of water. He then freed Bolac's left hand and said, "Now you can drink and be of good cheer, for you will not meet death for some time to come. Now forgive me, I must now take my leave."

Bolac thought, I must conserve my strength, for certainly, I shall die if this devil continues to take my blood. At last, sleep came to him. The following evening, Dracula returned and repeated the grizzly ritual. After drinking the last drop from the cup, he smiled and said, "You must be hungry."

Once again, he departed and soon returned with a potato, carrot, and beef. "Now eat," he ordered, "for you are looking pale."

"Please give me something to cover my body for I am quite cold." Dracula replied with a blow to Bolac's temple.

"Now if you will pardon me, I have other matters to attend to." But his wit was wasted on the unconscious Bolac. Ten minutes after his tormentor had gone, Bolac returned to his senses. He saw that he was alone and greedily ate the vegetables that had been brought to him. Feeling somewhat better, he began to think to escape. He began by examining the chain that held his wrists. Thanks to the candles, he was able to see quite well. He noticed that his shackle was very rusty and began to pull with all the strength that he possessed. After twenty minutes, he had no strength to continue. Thirty minutes later, he resumed, and this time his efforts bore fruit as the wedge began to yield. For the next fourteen hours, he pulled and twisted every twenty minutes of the hour. Exhausted and spent, he fell into a deep sleep. He dreamed of the riches he would never have. The dream was interrupted as he felt the hairs of his head literally being torn out.

"I see you have eaten. Now it is my turn." After two hours of agonizing torment, his antagonist departed. But this time he did not return with food and water. Bolac knew that he would soon die. He also knew that before he began to pull at the chain, he must have sleep.

CHAPTER II

THE ABDUCTION

Anna and Marie sat up in their beds, full of excitement as they discussed Marie's upcoming wedding. "Just think, Marie, three days from now, you will be spending your first night with Carl. Do you think you will miss sleeping with me?"

"In two years, you also will be seventeen, and after your wedding night, you can ask yourself the same question. Now let us go to sleep before our chatter awakens the household."

As the two sisters slept, the room began to slowly fill with a mist. It began to take form, and in a moment the metamorphosis was complete—the cold hazel eyes, full of lust, searching the faces of the two sisters. One was more beautiful than the other. Marie, lying with her breast exposed, brought delight to the eyes of the beholder. He reached down and picked her up ever so gently and carried her through the house and out the door, his thoughts full with the pleasure she would give him.

Now he must hurry to return to the castle, since the sun would rise in two hours. Marie opened her eyes, thinking it was a dream, and her husband-to-be had come to carry her off before the wedding day, because he could wait no longer to posses her. The dream was shattered as she looked into the face of her abductor. She screamed the scream of one who had gone mad instantly. Looking at her terror-stricken face, he knew that would be the last sound she would make for some time to come. By the time he arrived at the castle, the sun had begun to burn away the night. Must I go through eternity with the accursed light challenging my very being? he thought as he entered his room and dropped Marie to the floor. He himself lay on his bed and fell into a deathlike sleep.

Bolac, with his last ounce of strength, pulled the chain from the wall. His right arm was useless, having supported his body during his sleeping hours. He could not find the key to free the lock and chain from around his wrist, so he looped it around his neck and fashioned a sling for his useless arm.

Now, he thought, he must find clothing to cover his shivering body. With only one candle remaining, he proceeded to light his way. After he had taken several steps, he came upon the treasury room. "Yes, I will find clothing. Karva, if he is still here, will have no need for his. If only I had taken heed of his fear, he and I would have been better off." He went inside and saw Karva's fleshless remains. The rats were still gnawing at the bones. Sick to his stomach, he stumbled out. His first thought was to run, but he knew that he must conserve his energy. Also, he did not want to make a sound. If he should encounter this madman, his life would be at an end. Once at the top of the stairs, he listened for any sound of movement. There was none. He wondered if this devil could be asleep. And if so, did he have the strength to kill him? Well, he thought, if there is clothing, I will find them upstairs.

He found clothing in the first room. He could see at a glance they were quite old but, nonetheless, far better than anything he had ever owned. Dressing hastily, he looked into all the bedchambers until he came upon the sleeping form of his tormentor. He thought of wrapping the chain around his neck and choking the life out of him. But he could not bring himself to approach him because he had begun to paralyze in fear. He saw the pathetic girl lying on the floor and thought she was dead. As he was about to close the door, she moved her head ever so slightly. Without thinking, he took hold of her arm and dragged her out. Once outside, the cold morning air began to revive her. She opened her eyes and said, "Please, don't harm me."

"Be still," he replied, "you foolish girl, I'll not harm you. I have snatched you from the clutches of that demon. Now try to walk. We must flee from his place if we are to save our lives."

After arriving home safely, Marie found her family in panic. "What happened to you, and where have you been?" asked Marco, her father. Her mother was too hysterical to say anything. All she could do was to take the now-tearful Marie in her arms and hold her. She could not answer her father and looked to Bolac. He was too exhausted to explain. The father, sensing that Bolac was near collapse, instructed his sons to help him into the house.

He was no stranger to the household. They knew him as a thief and possibly a murderer. Bolac was given food and drink and was allowed to rest. After two hours of fitful sleep, he told of his ordeal of horror. This was the first time he had told the truth, with the exception that he blamed Karva for forcing him to take part in the scheme to enter the castle in search of riches.

Upon examination of his body, there was no choice but to believe his every word. Marco said, "We must report this. Bolac, you will go with me and tell your story to the constable. You will rest here for the night, and we will leave at first light." Bolac refused, saying, "I fear this demon will return here, and we are no match for him." "Surely, man, with my four strong young sons and myself, we should be more than able to defend ourselves against this so-called demon who I think is just a madman. But if you insist, you are free to go," said Marco.

"Father," Marie said in a surprisingly calm manner, "I fear to stay. I think we should all leave here at once."

"Nonsense," replied Marco, "you will be safe."

"Please, Father, I cannot stay! I beg you, let us leave." Marco, seeing that his daughter was distraught and may become hysterical, offered no further resistance. Turning to Bolac, he said, "I owe you much more than I can pay for saving the life of my daughter. I pray that you will do one last thing for me. Take my wife and two daughters with you to the village."

Anna, the mother, refused, pleading, "I will not leave my home. But Marie and little Anna may go."

"Hurry then," said Bolac, "I want to be in the village before nightfall."

"You may take the horse and cart," said Marco. "You will be in the village long before dark. Take my daughters to the house of the priest and tell him I will call for them tomorrow if this business is done with. And again, I thank you, Bolac." Twenty minutes after a tearful farewell, Bolac and his two charges were on their way.

Screaming obscenities, Dracula ran through the castle in search of his captives, causing the rats to scurry about; those caught under his heels were crushed to a pulp. Realizing his efforts are fruitless, he ran out into the darkness, shouting into the night, "So the two pathetic mortals think they can escape me and find safety!"

The winged messenger of death circled the home of Marco. While inside, Anna asked her husband, "Do you think he will come?"

"I don't know. But if so, we are prepared to defend ourselves."

The eldest son said, "We shall take turns at watch through the night." Then he added to reassure his mother, "We each have an axe, and we are more than a match against this crazed man."

Just as Marco was about to agree with his son, the door left its hinges as if struck by a bolt of lightning. Carl, the younger of the sons, reacted first. Leaping to his feet and picking up the axe by his side, he swung with all his strength at the menacing figure before him. With catlike reflexes, Dracula raised his left arm and caught the instrument inches before it found its target. He pulled the boy to him and turned him to a forty-five-degree angle.

Marco and his oldest son, seizing the opportunity, lifted their axes and struck. With a twist of his wrist, Dracula placed the young boy in the path of the oncoming axes which struck the boy between the shoulder blades. Tossing the now-dead boy aside, but holding onto his axe, with one mighty swing, he served the head of Marco. Anna screamed with such force that the blood vessels in her throat ruptured, and within minutes, she choked to death on her own blood.

The two remaining brothers, half-crazed with anger, threw themselves with such force at the leering figure that he was knocked off his feet. They hammered with their fists with all their might. Dracula, shocked temporarily at their subhuman strength, quickly transformed to the four-legged beast from hell and speedily dispatched the two young men.

After searching in vain for Marie, he mused that henceforth he would control himself. Had he not killed them all, he would have gotten information on the whereabouts of Marie and her champion. However, be that as it may, he would seek them out and return them from whence they escaped. Now, as he looked at the torn bodies about him, he thirsted; it was time to fill his need. Tomorrow evening he would go into the village and reclaim the girl and the would-be thief.

CHAPTER 12

THE INVESTIGATION

"I have sent for you, Captain, for I want you to listen to a most remarkable story," said Father Raymond, as the big policeman entered the study of the rectory. "Of course you know my three visitors."

"Yes," replied the captain. "This one, all too well," he added, looking at Bolac. "And pray tell, Father Raymond, what are the likes of him doing here and in the company of these two lovely flowers?"

"Please be seated, Captain, and you, my son," said Father Raymond to Bolac, "repeat what you have already told me."

Bolac objected, "I am tired and wish to leave." As he attempted to rise from his chair, the priest put his hand on Bolac's shoulder.

"There is no place to go if you fear for your life, and I know you do. You must remain here."

Bolac looked up at the face of the man bending over him and knew his efforts to resist were hopeless. Father Raymond was an imposing man, not quite as large as the captain, but his six-foot three-inch, one-hundred-ninety-pound frame seemed to loom over the captain's six-foot six-inch body. In fact, in most of his fifty years of life, all those who came in contact with him had felt it was useless to oppose him, not through fear, but from the intellect that emanated from him.

He had joined the priesthood thirty years ago, and he was a handsome young man of twenty, with a full head of overly long black hair, when he had taken his vows. He chose to shave it off in honor of his teacher and mentor who took him in hand when he first entered the seminary at the age of sixteen. He also would not let his hair grow, often jesting with his young student, saying, "Keep nothing on your head so that my words of wisdom may penetrate." Raymond did become a brilliant student.

After Bolac and Marie finished relating the events that led to their presence, Anna could only attest to the condition of the two upon their arrival. "It is an amazing tale, but I cannot bring myself to believe it. I do believe Marie and the fact that she was taken from her bed, but as for Bolac, the truth from him is unfamiliar as is an honest day's work. But, nonetheless, I will look into the matter."

"Pardon, Captain," said Father Raymond, "but I do not believe you fully understand the significance of what we have been told. As for Bolac, I firmly believe that he did tell the truth. Look at his face and wrist. But the most interesting part of his story is the drinking of his blood."

"Be that as it may," replied the captain, "it means there is a madman on the loose."

"Tell me, Captain, do you remember the stories of the murders some eighty years ago?"

"Yes, in fact, I read the records several years ago. But what are you saying?" "Well, I too have read the old records during the course of some research of a book I read at the monastery about twenty-five years ago. I do not understand," continued Father Raymond, "how could that be related to what has happened to Bolac? Surely you are not suggesting that the same madman is alive?"

"Why, Father, he would well be a hundred years old or more. Besides, there has not been a murder of any such kind. Now, it is late. I will leave in the morning and go see Marco."

"Excuse me, sir, my father said he would come to take us home tomorrow," said Marie.

"Very good," replied the captain, "have him come to my office when he arrives. Now I bid you all good night."

"I will see you to the door, Captain," Bolac offered.

Before the two men left the room, Father Raymond said, "I did not want to alarm the others, but allow me to explain why I believe Bolac has told the truth. Do you recall what he said? When he and Karva approached the treasury room there was no lock, and to gain entry they only had to remove a cross."

"Yes, Father, but I do not understand."

"I will explain. The cross was left there as a seal not for the purpose of keeping anyone out, but to keep someone in. Of course, any God-fearing man, seeing the cross, would not have removed it. I have read the account of why it had been placed there. That is why I charged that you did not fully grasp the significance of the matter in question."

"Father, please, I will investigate fully the entire matter. You have my word. Now, I must say goodnight."

"One more thing, Captain, before you take your leave. The cross was placed there by Saint Francis of Assisi. I suggest that you do not wait for Marco to come."

"All right, Father. I will go to him. I will leave early in the morning, and perhaps I will meet him on the road. Now may I leave?"

The priest pressed his point further, "I fear you will be too late."

"Come now, Father Raymond, Marco has four strong young sons," replied the captain, his patience now at an end. "I will see you when I return." The two men shook hands, and at last, the captain departed.

Before returning to his study, Father Raymond summoned his housekeeper and asked her to prepare food for his guests. After they had eaten, he announced that it was time for them to be taken to their rooms. He himself would do without sleep, for he prayed through the night.

True to his word, the captain, with his corporal, rode out to question Marco. They arrived a little after sunset.

"Look!" shouted the corporal as they approached the house. "There is no door." Climbing down from their horses, the men stood for a moment, examining the door frame.

"It looks as though it was struck by a battering ram," said the captain. "Come, let us investigate." As they entered, the smell of death was overpowering, and it attacked their nostrils even before they could comprehend the ghastly sight before them. Both men faltered as their knees buckled. The captain threw himself to the wall for support. The corporal stood his ground until he had finished urinating. He then turned and fled. Moments later, Captain Wycoff stood by the side of the weeping young man.

"I am sorry, sir, please forgive me."

"Do not apologize, my friend, you are only human."

"Sir, what kind of animal could do such a thing? I fear it was not an animal as such, but something more akin to human."

"I do not understand. I am not sure I do, Corporal," said the captain, "but if my fears are correct, Father Raymond will supply the answers. Now I must leave. You remain here. I will return as soon as I can."

CHAPTER 13

CARNAGE

The two men looked down at the delirious and shaking body of Bolac. "I have done all I can," said the doctor. "I am afraid the infection is too far advanced. Also, the fever is much too high. He will not last out the day. Tell me, Father, how was such a wound inflicted?"

Father Raymond related the story as told by Bolac and Marie. The doctor listened in mute silence. After which, he asked, "Surely, Father, you don't believe such a tale? Why, the poor wretched soul must have been more than half mad with fever."

"No, my friend, the story he told was not the utterance of a madman. Look at the condition of his body; also, Marie can attest, somewhat, to the fact of where they were. Perhaps, we shall learn more when Captain Wycoff returns."

"Father, I have the feeling that you know more than you have said."

"Be patient, Doctor, soon you will learn all that I know. It will take our combined efforts, with the help of God, to put an end to the nightmare that began some eighty years ago."

"Forgive me," said the doctor, "but are you referring to the tales that the old woman told when we were children? Father, I am a man of science and you are a man of learning. Surely you are not taken in by the superstition that one prevailed upon our land?"

"Only time will tell, Doctor. Come, let us see to the young ladies." Father Raymond instructed his housekeeper to attend to Bolac and to inform them of any change in his condition. Then the two men entered the kitchen where they found Marie and Anna, who had just finished breakfast.

Captain Wycoff arrived at the church, his horse totally spent. He did not remember ever riding with such energy in his life. As the two men faced each other, Father Raymond knew that his fears had become a reality. Before Wycoff could speak, Father Raymond suggested the doctor and the captain accompany him to his study. Marie asked the captain if he had seen her father. The captain took the priest aside and whispered simply that the entire family was found dead upon their arrival.

"Captain, would you and the good doctor be so kind as to await me in my study?" He then led Marie and Anna to the chapel. Fifteen minutes later, he left the two sisters softly crying in each other's arms.

He then joined the two waiting men in his study. Captain Wycoff gave a detailed and accurate account of what he had seen. The two men listened in stunned silence, and the doctor, who had been standing, found it necessary to seat himself. By the time Wycoff had finished his report, all were visibly shaken. The doctor, looking from one to the other, asked, "What can we do?" Wycoff spoke first, in a tone clearly denoting his professionalism.

"I will take eight or ten men and go to the castle to find this fiend and bring him back to face the justice of the people. Or, if necessary, he will meet his end on the spot by way of my sword."

"If you will pardon me, my friend, we will be dealing with a force whose powers we cannot even begin to comprehend. But do not despair," Father Raymond announced, sliding a book from his shelf. "This, gentlemen, is a copy of the original I had read many years ago of the works of St. Francis and Father Paul."

"I don't understand," interrupted the doctor, "I have heard the stories as a child of the visit of Francis of Assisi here in Transylvania, and that was almost a hundred years ago. Even if the stories are true, what does that have to do with the murder of Marco and his family? Who is that we have to apprehend now?"

"Bear with me," replied Father Raymond, "I do think the word 'apprehend' is not quite suitable. But to answer your question, Doctor, as to who—he is a product of hell, a part man and part devil. Yes, my friend, after eighty years, he is free again to stalk mankind. And as for the how, it is written that the destruction of this subhuman creature can be brought about by several means. First, by driving a wooden stake through his heart; second, by preventing him access to shelter during the daylight hours; third, by using fire as an effective means for his destruction. Now, as to the protection of oneself from physical attack, possess a crucifix or display the Holy Eucharist before his eyes and recite the Lord's Prayer. Lastly, and I fear the most difficult one, being in a state of holy grace. And those, gentlemen, are the alternatives, and I regret there are no other options afforded us. And yet, thanks to St. Francis and Father Paul, we have the knowledge to defend ourselves and send this lost soul to Hades."

"Pardon, Father," said the doctor, "as you are aware, I am not Catholic but a man of medicine and science, and although I am familiar with the dogma of the church, I am at a loss. Would you please explain what is meant by a 'state of grace'?"

"I too must confess my stupidity," interjected Wycoff.

"Forgive me," replied the priest, "I will explain. To achieve a state of grace is to renew the heart and restrain from sin and enter a state reconciled to God."

Wycoff and the doctor sat lost in their own thoughts, thinking of all that had been said. To Wycoff, it was the only thing that made sense, since he had read the reports of the killings of eighty years ago and, only an hour before, had seen the torn bodies of Marco and his sons. The doctor knew that it was medically impossible, so after all he had heard, he could reach only one conclusion—that he would have to see to believe.

Their thoughts were interrupted by the frantic knocking and shouting at the door by the housekeeper.

"Yes, what is it?" the priest asked, opening the door.

"The sick one. I cannot hold him down. I think he is fighting death."

"Doctor, if you please, follow me and let us see if we can be of some comfort to this unfortunate soul," said Father Raymond. As the two men left the room along with the housekeeper, Wycoff called out that he would be leaving to get men and start for the castle.

"Be sure to come back for me," replied the priest. His words fell on deaf ears as Wycoff was preoccupied with his own thoughts. As they entered the bedroom, they found Bolac on the floor. The two men lifted him and placed him on the bed.

"It is the fever," said the doctor. "I am afraid there is little time left for him." An hour and a half later, Bolac opened his eyes and said in a weak but clear voice, "Father, pray for me. Ask God to forgive me."

"I have already done so, my son." And then, there was stillness in the room, that which only death can cause.

"Well, Father, do you think God has forgiven him?" asked the doctor.

"I believe it to be so. Bolac's last act was one of unselfishness. He did save Marie."

Suddenly, without warning, Father Raymond took hold of the doctor and shouted, causing the physician to think the priest had taken leave of his sense, "Please tell me how long it has been since Wycoff has left us?" Then seeing the look of astonishment on the face of his friend, he immediately released him and offered his apology.

"About an hour and a half," answered the doctor.

"Come, my friend, there is not a moment to lose." Before leaving, he gave instructions to his housekeeper that under no circumstances was she to permit Marie or Anna to leave the sanctuary of the rectory. He then took from his desk a rosary and, giving it to the doctor, said, "Place this around your neck." The doctor did as he was told. To protest would be fruitless. Several minutes later, having learned that Wycoff had left with twenty-five men on their way to the castle, they too were in the doctor's carriage, on their way to the castle of Count Dracula. "We shall first stop at the home of Marco as it is on our way. I pray we find Captain Wycoff and the other men there."

"Why do you think they may be there?" asked the doctor.

"Because it is the halfway point, and they would surely stop to rest their horses."

Wycoff and his volunteers arrived at the farm of the unfortunate victims. He ordered the men to dismount and rest their horses. He then walked over to the corporal and briefly told of his plan to search the castle where he believed he would find the killer. "But why so many men?" asked the corporal.

"I will explain later," said Wycoff. "I also would like you to remain here until my return." Several of the men entered the house. When the others saw the look of terror on their faces, even though they were already aware of the deaths of the inhabitants, they felt that they were not prepared to face a visible inspection. Captain Wycoff told the men only of the deaths of Marco and his family, with the exception of the two daughters, stating that a fiend was responsible for the foul deed and that there was a good reason to believe that the murderer was hiding in the abandoned castle of Dracula.

He did not mention what he had heard from Father Raymond. He thought it best not to do so and arouse their superstitions. He then ordered several of the men to dig graves, telling them to place the bodies in them upon their return. Soon after, they were on their way, determined more to apprehend the crazed killer. The doctor and Father Raymond stopped at the open graves. The corporal hurriedly walked over to the two men, greatly relieved by their company. "I see by the tracks Captain Wycoff and the men were here," stated the priest as the corporal approached the carriage.

"Yes," replied the young man, "they rode off more than an hour ago."

"Please prepare two mounts for us," said the priest. Hoping he could persuade the two men to stay, the corporal volunteered that the captain and his men would return in a few hours.

"No, my son, it is imperative that I get to them as soon as possible. Come, Doctor, let us enter, and you shall see the demon's handiwork."

As they surveyed the carnage before them, Dr. Agreas was the first to speak. "Father, I quite agree nothing human could be responsible for this. It must be the work of some wild beast."

"Oh, come now, Doctor, what kind of animal do you know that could have done this? Look for yourself, there are no claw marks on any of the bodies." The priest took from his satchel a bottle of oil, poured a little on each of the victims, and said a short prayer. "They are in God's hands. Let us depart. The corporal should have the horses ready by now."

The corporal watched as the two rode away. He was in wonderment as to why Father Raymond had given him a cross and ordered him not to let it leave his hands, saying only that his life may depend on it.

Captain Wycoff and the men stopped their horses within twenty feet of the castle. It was less than an hour to sunset. A feeling of apprehension showed on their faces. The castle loomed ominously before them, the sight of which sent shivers down their spines. It seemed as if their horses were frozen in their tracks as the men looked to Wycoff for directions. Wycoff gave the order to dismount. There suddenly appeared at the open door of the castle a jackal. A few seconds later, it was followed by another, and then another and another until there were forty jackals in all. Saliva dripped from their mouths as they bared their teeth. The men were panic stricken. The horses reared and pulled. The men found it impossible to control them. The jackals attacked. The youngest of the soldiers, a boy of eighteen, was the first to meet his death. The crazed animal leaped at his victim. The boy raised his arms as if to catch the jackal in midair, but the beast slipped between his arms and took hold of his throat and bit with such force that his teeth interlocked. Wycoff, who had been standing less than four feet away, extended his arm, holding his sword, and lunged. The point of the blade entered the rectum of the beast a full twelve inches, and still, it did not release its hold. Not until Wycoff twisted his sword and pulled it free did it release its grip.

The next man to fall was a blacksmith, the largest of them all. Five jackals charged him. The first to reach him leaped for his throat, but the big man turned slightly, raised his arm, and protected his throat. The animal's razor-sharp teeth bit into the man's jowls. With one violent motion, he pulled the beast from his face, tearing half of his flesh away in the process. As the big man began to strangle the jackal, another leaped on his back, and still two others bit into the calves of his legs while a fourth clamped its viselike jaws into his testicles. The other men were in similar predicaments.

In order to regroup, the jackals retreated. And after a few minutes, they renewed their attack. The battle raged between man and beast, and by sunset there stood only Wycoff and five of his men. The rest lay torn and dead amongst the thirty-one slain jackals. Suddenly, from out of the top of the castle flew a large black bat, casting its shadow on the ground below as it circled the area. Just as the bat was about to attack Captain Wycoff, Father Raymond rode up and dismounted with his arm extended, holding a cross and shouting, "Be gone, Satan." The bat instantly began to flutter, but it somehow managed to fly away into the forest and the cover of darkness. The remaining jackals followed suit.

The doctor was the first to speak. "Father, I have seen, and I believe."

"Doctor, please see to the men. There may be some still alive, although I don't think so," said Wycoff. With the help of the priest and the other men, Wycoff's suspicions were confirmed.

"What do we do now?" asked the doctor of Father Raymond.

"Bury our dead," said the priest sadly.

"Yes," agreed Wycoff, "let us collect the horses so that we may carry the men." It took three hours before the task was completed. Before they left, the priest, with the help of the doctor, erected a cross at the front of the castle.

It was near dawn when the weary men arrived at Marco's. The ride had been slow and tedious. Several times, many of the bodies slipped from the backs of the horses. The men, in their haste to depart, had failed to secure the bonds that would have prevented mishaps.

The corporal had just awakened after a fitful sleep of a mere three hours when he heard the sounds of horses. He rubbed his eyes and had difficulty understanding Wycoff's brief report. The captain, seeing the dazed look upon the face of his subordinate, struck him with his open palm and shouted, "Now go and ring the death knell and return with the villagers so that they may pay their final respects to their loved ones and neighbors." As the young man prepared to mount his horse, Wycoff walked to him and, placing his hand on the shoulder of the embarrassed man, said very softly, "Please pardon me." Wycoff then turned and spoke to the men, "We need rest, but first let us remove the bodies from the horses and place them in the graves. I do not wish to have anyone else see them."

After the sickening task had been completed, the doctor cleaned and dressed the wounds of the men. The corporal returned in less than four hours with several hundred people. By noon the graves were dug and the dead were laid to rest. The mourners wept as the priest recited the Lord's Prayer. After he completed the services, Father Raymond asked that all remain. Having noticed that a dozen of the leading citizens had gathered around Wycoff, he walked over to them as Wycoff attempted to explain his actions to the angry men. "Would you have us believe in goblins and the like?" asked the mayor in a soft, quizzical voice as though he were speaking to a child. All eyes were on Wycoff as he flustered with anger. He stepped closer to the mayor, their faces just six inches apart, and asked through clenched teeth, "Would you have me unearth the bodies of Marco and his family?" The mayor cowered as the captain's eyes bore into him, and he quickly stepped back for he feared he would be physically attacked.

Father Raymond walked into the center of the men and said, "I can assure you what the captain has told you is true. Also, the doctor can bear witness as to the conditions of the deceased, as well as the corporal."

The mayor, having regained his composure, being the politician that he was, was the first to reply. "Father, you cannot fault us for not believing that Count Dracula is still alive and responsible for this crime. Might it not be just some madman attempting to emulate this Dracula of so long ago? And what of the people? Should they hear of this, they will surely panic. I am afraid we have no choice but to tell them so they may be able to protect themselves."

"We are not left unprotected," said the priest, "thanks to God's mercy. Now go among the people and gather them in groups of twenty-five or so. Tell them to return to their homes and place a crucifix on their doors and under no circumstances are they to venture out of doors after sundown. Hurry now, for we have much to do."

The men departed and did as they were told.

"What are we going to do?" asked Wycoff. The priest suggested that men be sent to the countryside to give warning to the inhabitants.

"Now I must return to the rectory. Captain, I will see you and the mayor as well as the doctor at sunrise in my office."

As the doctor and Father Raymond walked toward the carriage, Wycoff called the priest aside and asked, "Do you really think we can overcome this creature? I have seen a little of the awesome powers he possesses."

"You are right, Captain, he does have great powers, and we must not err again in our judgment."

"What do you mean, 'again'?"

"I must admit that I am guilty. First, I allowed you to leave from the castle without me, and second, I placed a cross at the castle to prevent Dracula from entering. Had I not done so, we would know his whereabouts during the daylight hours. Now he will take refuge elsewhere."

"Father, it is I who have the blood of the men on my hands. For I did hear you call after me to return for you. I thought I could destroy that devil without help. How foolish."

Father Raymond placed his hands on his shoulders and looked into the tearful eyes of his friend. "We all have our crosses to bear, but you will find that if you ask in prayer, in time, the burden will be lifted." And with that, the two men parted.

Upon his arrival, Father Raymond was pleased after being informed by his housekeeper that Carl had arrived an hour ago and was with Marie and Anna in the church garden. Carl, Marie's husband-to-be, was a young man of twenty and of medium height, five feet seven inches. His face looked as though it had been chiseled out of rock, with square cut jaws; he looked older than his twenty years. When nervous, he had a certain way of placing his hand on top of his head and very slowly moving it through a shock of thick, curly black hair, which made him appear quite boyish. He was a bright young man with a fairly good education, having spent the last two years of his schooling in the monastery. He realized that his true vocation was the life of a farmer and that his heart belonged to Marie, so he left the monastery.

After being at the gravesite of Marie's parents, and now sitting with the girls, he thought what a black day it had been. He had awakened a little before sun up, full of expectation of visiting his betrothed. He had a full hour of work completed by the time his father and brothers had come to help with their share of the work. It had been agreed that he could leave well before noon to see Marie. He arrived just as Corporal Kostal led the villagers to Marco's property. After being told that Marie and Anna were safe and their whereabouts by Dr. Agress, he mounted his horse and rode off moments after Father Raymond had given the final blessing at the gravesite.

"Come sit, the food is ready, I will call our guest," said the housekeeper. After they had eaten, Carl announced that he would take Marie and Anna home with him.

"I am sorry, Carl, but that is quite impossible," replied the priest. "I want to thank you for taking care of Marie and Anna, but I can take care of them now. You do not understand the situation, Carl. I will explain if you will follow me to my study." After informing him of the events that transpired over the last several days, the priest then asked him if he fully understood why Marie must not leave.

"I am not sure. I'd like everyone to know of the legend of Dracula, but I will do as you ask. Now I must return home."

"No, Carl, darkness will soon be upon us. You must remain here for your own safety."

"Father, how can we put an end to his evil?"

"We shall discuss the matter fully tomorrow morning. Now I must have rest. Oh, yes, Captain Wycoff has sent someone to warn your family and to tell them how best to protect themselves as well as your neighbors. If you like, after you have bid goodnight to Marie and Anna, you may read this book. It will help you understand that, with which we must deal." Father Raymond then went into the church to pray for guidance and strength to face the ordeal ahead.

The stranger entered the inn. One could plainly see he was an aristocrat. The inn was filled with seamen. Two ships had just come into port. His appearance drew the attention of all. But as he seated himself, he singled out one of the three plump serving girls and ordered drinks for everyone. Upon learning of the generosity of the stranger, their scrutiny ceased. He ordered bread and cheese for himself.

"Pardon, sir, I would like to thank you for the rum for myself and these other louts who seem to have forgotten their manners. Permit me to introduce myself. I am Captain Manay, and I am master of the vessel, *Lunar*, at your service."

"Have you been in port long, Captain?" asked the stranger.

"No, only since this morning. My crew has just completed unloading our cargo."

"Then you will be setting sail soon?"

"Yes, when we collect another cargo."

"Allow me to have another round brought over."

"Thank you, sir, may I have the honor of knowing the name of so generous a person?"

"I am your employer, Captain, and I am here to commission you to pick up some cargo for me. I presume you're sailing for France?"

"Yes," replied Captain Manay. Taking out his purse and removing five pearls, the stranger placed them in the hand of the wide-eyed captain.

"Now, this is what you must do. You are to purchase three oxen and carts and go to my estate and pick up my property, nine trunks in all. I will give you a map so that you may not have difficulty finding your way. I will see you on the third day at your vessel, and there I will pay you five more of the same. I will give you further instructions before we set sail." He then put a gold coin on the table and was about to take his leave when as if in afterthought he said, "Captain, you will find a cross at the entrance of my castle. See that you destroy it."

"Pardon, Captain," said the first mate, as he slowly lowered himself into the chair beside Manay. "May I ask of whom you were speaking to?"

"Why?" asked the captain.

"I don't know, except I could not help but look as you were talking, and a strange feeling overwhelmed me. I could not reason why until I looked into the man's face as he was leaving."

"Well, out with it," interrupted Manay.

"Well, sir, I have served these many years, and we have been through the thick of it, but not until this very night have I known fear." Reluctant to admit his own apprehension, the captain replied, "Nonsense, he has just commissioned the *Lunar*, and we have work to do. We leave tomorrow. Collect five of our strongest from the crew."

"May I ask our destination?"

"Into the mountains," answered the captain, barely able to keep his hand from shaking as he lifted the cup of rum to his mouth.

Ten seconds after he had closed the door of the inn and stepped into the night, a man who had been observing from a nearby table watched with great interest as Dracula removed the gold coin from his heavily laden purse. He decided that he would relieve the stranger of his heavenly burden, so he followed him under the cover of darkness. With quick strides, he overtook the shadowy figure before him. He removed from his waistband his sack that he knew with one blow would render his victim unconscious or worse. It did not matter to him so long as he could possess more gold than he had ever had before. But his dreams of riches were shattered as his would-be prey suddenly turned, and he found himself frozen in the hypnotic eyes of his would-be victim.

His knees buckled, and the sack slipped from his hand as the sight of the face before him sent waves of shudders throughout his body. After what seemed like an eternity, he heard the stranger ask, "Are you seeking employment or death? Speak," demanded Dracula.

The would-be thief heard himself answering, "Only to serve you, master."

"Your choice is a wise one," Dracula said to the visibly shaken man standing before him, twitching at his left ear, which was most unusual, due to the fact that the ear had been bitten off several years before in a drunken brawl. Dracula placed two gold coins in the man's hand and told him to purchase a horse and ride him into the village. There he would secure lodging at the inn and remain there until he called on him.

Count Dracula, feeling quite pleased with himself, walked toward the ships, six in all. Then he came upon two seamen, appearing very drunk, with one helping the other. A closer inspection would reveal that the two had been in a fight. The smaller of the two was bleeding profusely through the nostrils, and his right eye was no more than mere slit. The taller one had a five-inch gash that laid his right cheekbone bare. They had gotten into an argument concerning which one would spend the night with one of the serving girls at the inn. Needless to say, while they engaged in combat, a third shipmate of theirs made off with the prize.

They approached the waiting figure, expecting him to step aside from the narrow walkway. He held his ground. The taller one raised his arm to push Dracula aside. Dracula, seeing the bloody faces of the men, went amuck. The two were grabbed by the throat, and minutes later, his thirst gratified, he turned and disappeared into the night. He left the bodies of the two unfortunates in a grotesque heap where they once stood.

Captain Wycoff, the mayor, and the doctor arrived almost at the same time at Father Raymond's church. As they were about to begin to discuss what was to be done to eliminate once again the curse that had returned to Transylvania, they were joined by Carl, who seated himself next to the doctor. The doctor inquired about the welfare of the two girls.

"They are sleeping, for we talked far into the night."

"It is just as well. The rest is better than all the medicine I have at my disposal."

"Now, then," asked Father Raymond, "are we all in agreement that the danger is present and real?" His eyes rested on the mayor. The mayor, feeling somewhat uneasy, answered, "Yes, Father, the doctor and Wycoff gave me a complete report."

"Very good. I have given the matter much thought. We must allow him to reenter the castle. Therefore, I must return and remove the cross. And after he has returned, I will, with the help of God, seek him out and put an end to his existence."

"You make it sound so simple, and why do you think he will return to the castle?" asked the mayor.

"I don't know, only the fact that it is his home. We could search the mountains and forest for him, but our chances of success would be no less than a minimum. Now, my friends, I am ready to leave."

"You are not going alone. I will, of course, go with you," said Wycoff, "and I suggest I bring as many men that are willing to go."

"Thank you, Captain, eight men should be enough to search the castle."

"I too will go," Carl offered.

"No, Carl, you must stay and look after the girls. It may be several days before we return. Therefore, we must take provisions."

"I will see to it, Father," the mayor said.

"Thank you, Mayor."

"It will take two hours before we are ready, Father, and we should arrive at the castle well after dark. Do you not think it will be to our advantage to arrive at sun up?" the captain suggested.

"Yes, I agree. We shall camp in the forest a mile or so from the castle," Father Raymond answered.

"Why don't you wait inside?" asked Carl.

"I trust he would be aware of our presence, and therefore, our mission would meet with defeat.

After a hearty meal of pork, potatoes, cheese, and bread, washed down with a mug of wine, he sat in his room wondering what was expected of him in the way of employment. Of course, his plan was simple. Once he had gained the trust of the stranger, it would be easy to crack open his scull and make off with his wealth, of which he was certain to be considerable. His thoughts were interrupted by a rush of wind as the balcony doors were nearly torn off their hinges. For the second time in his life, he tasted fear as he looked once again at the face that caused his legs to turn to mush. He could not believe it when he heard himself asking, "What is it you would have me do, sir?"

The figure stepped out of the shadows where he had been standing and walked toward the side of the church. He slowly made his way to the door that led to the kitchen. Marie had decided it was time to busy herself. She had insisted that she be allowed to prepare the evening meal. Anna, unable to control the flood of tears that overcame her every hour or so, had just been led by the housekeeper to the bedroom. Carl had just locked the front doors of the church and returned to the kitchen to find the frail door open and Marie being lifted from the floor by the intruder. Carl, overcome with rage, leaped at the would-be abductor with such force that Marie was dropped to the floor. The intruder, with Carl on his back, recovered his balance. Violently twisting his body, he freed himself from Carl's grasp and caused him to knock over the kitchen table, crashing a bowl of grapes to the floor. Carl was on his feet in a split second, charging like a wild bull only to be met with a blow that had such force it broke his jaw along with four of his teeth. The pain caused momentary blindness. As he shook his head to clear his eyes, he felt his body being lifted and slammed into the opposite wall. Again, he heard the sound of breaking bones as his shoulder hit the wall, leaving his left arm completely useless.

"Now you die," shouted the attacker as he advanced for the kill. Carl forced himself to an upright position to protect himself from the onslaught, but it was not to come. The attacker lost his footing as he stepped on the fallen grapes. Carl, realizing this would be his only chance, reached down and took hold of the intruder's cloak and wrapped it around the fallen man's head. He then picked up the broken half of the wooden bowl and plunged it into the heart of the twisting body beneath him. The scream was ear shattering. Carl did not hear the scream as his mind and body fell into the blackness of pain-ridden sleep.

When he awakened, Dr. Agress was assuring Marie that Carl, with care, would be as good as new. The mayor was smiling as Carl's vision came into focus. "We are proud of you, Carl," he said.

"I am sorry, everyone must leave, this young man needs rest," said the doctor.

"May I stay?" Marie asked.

"Yes, Marie. See if you can get some broth to him. I must leave, for I have much to do."

"Tell me, Doctor, how long will it take before Carl is on his feet?" asked the mayor.

"Well, he is young and strong. I think two or three days," replied the doctor.

"Good, I will declare a feast to be held after their marriage," the mayor offered.

"Well, I think to be on the safe side, you should wait a week. Now I would like to see the body for a closer examination," stated the doctor.

"I had the body moved into the churchyard," said the mayor.

"What of Father Raymond and the other men?"

"I have sent two men after them to tell them the good news," replied the mayor.

"How can you be sure? No one has seen him and lived."

"I am well aware of that fact, Doctor. If you look at his cloak, you will see it bears the Dracula crest. When you have finished your examination, I will have him buried, since I cannot keep men on guard all day, and the crowd will be getting bigger and may get out of hand."

As the night gave way to the light of day, Father Raymond, Captain Wycoff, and the other men prepared to continue the last lap of their journey when the two messengers rode into their campsite with the news of the death of Dracula. The men accepted this statement with a sigh of relief. Now it would not be necessary to go to the castle.

"How did this come about?" asked the captain.

"All we can tell you, Captain, is that it was Carl who killed him when he came to take Marie."

The men mounted their horses to return to the village. Wycoff looked back to see that Father Raymond had not as yet mounted. He turned his horse around and rode back fifteen yards or so to where the priest stood and asked what was wrong.

"I do not know. I am just wondering if we should not do as we have planned."

"Come, let us leave this place. It would serve no purpose." Father Raymond agreed, with reluctance, as he mounted his horse.

CHAPTER 14

HE'S ALIVE

Five days later, Marie became Carl's wife. As they left the church, the mayor declared a holiday in honor of Carl, the bravest of the brave. As the festivities continued well after sunset, no one noticed that Carl and Marie had gone with Anna and Carl's parents. The doctor insisted that the couple leave, since Carl had not yet regained his full strength. Wycoff had offered an escort, but his gesture was declined. Then seeing Father Raymond standing alone, he walked to him and inquired as to why he was not enjoying the celebration. "Step inside, my friend, and have a glass of wine with me, and I will answer your question."

As Father Raymond led the way to his study, Wycoff's spirits changed from festive to somber. Realizing the seriousness in the tone of the voice of the priest, he now regretted having asked the question. After pouring the wine, Father Raymond said, "The man in the grave is not Dracula."

"How could you know that, Father?" asked Wycoff.

"Please listen," the priest continued, "you recall that when we returned a few days ago, we found that the body had been buried by order of the mayor?"

"Yes," answered Wycoff, "I know that since the doctor had declared him dead."

"That is true, but what disturbs me is how Carl could overcome him when Marco and his four sons could not save their own lives. So yesterday, I unearthed the body, and I am satisfied it isn't him. The left ear was missing, and according to the description of St. Francis, this could not be him."

"Maybe he did not notice the ear was missing," interjected Wycoff.

"I don't think so, but let me finish. I then poured holy water over the body, and nothing happened. I also placed a crucifix on his forehead and still nothing."

"Well, what did you expect to happen?" asked his friend.

"By the written words of St. Francis," Father Raymond continued, "his body would have reacted violently. And lastly, how could you explain the death of the two seamen, murdered in the same manner as the others? Now ask yourself, Captain, why was he at the seaport? To take passage on one of the ships, correct? And to find someone to enter the rectory, because he, himself, could not enter the house of God. But did he not want Marie? No. He knew that if he were successful, her abductor would be apprehended in due course and executed, thus having everyone believe that he had been destroyed. It would leave him free to move about in another land. You must remember that he is as clever as he is evil."

"But if what you say is true," said the captain, "then we are at last free of this demon. And although I agree with you; I think it best not to alert our countrymen. In any event, the danger has passed."

"Yes," said the priest, "for us, but let us pray for the land that will unwillingly host this son of the Prince of Darkness."

CHAPTER 15

THE VOYAGE

The *Lunar* made its way from Transylvania to its home port of Marseilles through stormy seas. The ship, however, remained intact with the exception of one mishap—the loss of three seamen while on night watch. The ship docked at 10:00 a.m. Captain Manay gave orders that the cargo was to be left untouched and no man was to remove the locks leading to the hold of ship until he returned. The first mate was perplexed by the captain's strange behavior.

"Sir, you are my captain, and I will obey your orders, but more important is the fact that we have been friends even before I first set foot aboard the *Lunar* as your first mate. And as a friend, I would like to ask if you do not think it odd that our passenger has not been seen during the day, and that he only ventures on deck at night. Also, I would like to mention the trip to that forbidden castle to fetch his belongings. And when we were lost, I am certain that a bat was following us and led us to the right path. And the cross at the entrance of the castle, why did we have to tear it down? Having done so, he appeared, shouting for us to step inside and remove the trunks, then locked us out so that we had to spend the rest of the night outdoors. And when we returned to the ship late in the evening, he was waiting. How was that possible when we left at sunrise while he remained in the castle?"

"I am sure there is an explanation to your questions," replied the captain, "but I do not have time to look for answers. Be satisfied that you and the men who accompanied me to the castle were paid a handsome sum. So let there be no more talk of our passenger. Now, I have business to attend. I will return as soon as I can, and stop worrying, my friend. Our journey is over, and in a few hours we shall indulge ourselves with wine and the daughters of France."

"One more thing, Captain," said the first mate, "the most significant of all is that the three men lost at sea were with us at the castle; therefore, they have no need for a bonus."

"I am sorry, I did not realize. Perhaps, you can see that their families receive the share, along with the wages. Now keep a watchful eye; I will return soon."

Nervously, he paced the deck. His anxiety increased with each passing hour. When, at last, after six hours, Captain Manay returned and called to his first mate to begin unloading the cargo stored in the first and second holes.

The sun dropped from sight on the horizon by the time the work had been completed. He then ordered the third hatch opened and had the nine trunks placed on the two waiting wagons.

"Shall I dismiss the men, sir?" asked the first mate.

"No, have the men stand by and summon our passenger," replied the captain.

"That won't be necessary," stated the first mate, "he is approaching us now."

"Good evening, sir," the captain greeted.

"Have you followed my instructions, Manay?"

"Yes, your possessions have been placed on the two wagons, and here are your keys and receipts. Your coach awaits you," answered the captain. "Now, sir, there only remains the balance of my payment."

"Yes, of course, Captain." He handed five pearls to the captain's awaiting hands. "Where can I contact you and the first mate if I have further need of your services?"

"I am afraid that would be impossible, sir, for we leave within the hour."

The captain continued, "May I suggest that you take your leave as it will be five hours until you arrive at your destination?"

Dracula was livid with rage and fought desperately to control himself as he turned on his heels and left the ship. Captain Manay walked over to his first mate, who had stepped back several feet during the exchange, and admitted that he was greatly relieved to be rid of this passenger. "Now you may dismiss the crew except for the night watch," he said.

"Pardon, sir, did I not overhear you say we were to set sail?"

"I lied, for I did not want him to know our whereabouts. While making my way back after completing his instructions, I began to think over your questions, and I do believe there is merit in your suspicions. But I was not sure until he asked where he could locate us. It was then I realized that we were in danger of losing our lives. Had he further need of my services, I alone as the captain would be the one to approve any future commissions. Therefore, had I given him the information, I would wager we too, before long, would have joined our missing crewmen in death, leaving none to tell of our journey to that God-forbidden castle. Although I cannot prove it, I am sure he is responsible for the disappearances of the men."

The first mate spoke, "Do you think he may come and look for us?"

"Not during the day," answered Manay. "For some reason he will not venture out during daylight. That is why I had to purchase his new castle. I gave a partial payment in jewels to the barrister who shall call on him tomorrow evening to complete the arrangements."

"Then, you must know his name," stated the first mate.

"That I do, lad. He is the most sinister-looking man that I have had the misfortune to meet, and I am certain you agree, someone we are not likely to forget. He calls himself Count Dracula."

"Will you enter all that had happened in the ship's log?" asked the mate.

"No, but I will in my diary."

Dracula indulged himself during the passing centuries. He could be found in the king's court, for he mingled only with the rich and powerful of France. Of course, no one noticed or paid attention to the twelve or fifteen mangled and bloodless bodies that turned up monthly, added to the sixty or so that were usually found amongst the rubble, since France was in constant state of civil disturbance.

He remained in his adopted country for a hundred years after which time he returned to his homeland to reclaim his estate. He hired a barrister to represent him, supplying him with the necessary documents and also to spare no expense for the refurbishing of the castle and grounds. This was done three years before his arrival there.

The population had more than tripled in the past hundred years. He also employed an army of Turks, 250 or more. They were allowed to have their women and children with them. He had also a staff of servants consisting of ten men and twenty women. He entertained lavishly, as many as a hundred at a time. The birth rate rose rapidly, providing him with a steady supply of victims. Since he was a reasonable man, he did not neglect a few houseguests now and then who had the misfortune of offending him in some slight manner.

After forty years, he returned to France, and fifty years later, he went to Germany, then to Russia and Italy, staying approximately fifty years in each. He also went to three or four other countries, and by the year 1850, he had completed the cycle several times.

CHAPTER 16

DESTROY THE FAITH

In 1521 Dracula arrived in the city of Rome to put into motion the most ambitious undertaking of his existence, and there was no doubt in his devious mind that he would be no less than victorious. He had taken residence as the guest of Raphael Colonna, a practitioner of the black arts, whom he met two years before in Germany.

Raphael was an extremely thin man, one hundred fifteen pounds, five feet nine inches in height. Although fifty-four years of age, he still possessed a full head of jet-black hair. His nearly lipless mouth exposed his blackened teeth. A wealthy man all his life, he indulged himself in the pleasures of the flesh. Now for the past six years, he found he could only obtain sexual gratification in the arms of young boys. His wealth assured him of a constant supply of the youthful bodies.

At the age of twenty-five, he began the practice of the black arts in search of immortality, and as yet he was still unable to make contact with the Prince of Darkness. His first meeting with Dracula was at a party given by a Byron Kruger in the city of Berlin. There were thirty guests in all, and by 10:00 p.m., the party had become a full-scale orgy of the kind for which Berlin was quite famous. No one bothered to seek privacy.

The naked bodies lay entangled on the floor of the spacious dining room. Raphael was astonished at the sexual prowess of the stranger who still appeared fresh and virile after having exhausted half a dozen women. By 4:00 a.m., Raphael was the only one watching the stranger, who for the past three hours greedily possessed one woman after the next. He sat spent as the object of his attention stood up on his feet and retrieved his cape and observed the motionless bodies that lay about the floor. Smiling, he turned and focused his gaze at the seated naked, skeletonlike form, saying, "It is a pity that I must depart."

Raphael, filled with emotion, responded, "I would give my soul if I possessed your stamina. Never have I witnessed what I have seen this night. Tell me, sir, what matter of drug do you take?" Dracula removed from his vest pocket a small gold box and exposed its contents. Raphael's eyes widened as he inspected the white powder held before him. Dracula instructed him in the use of the substance. Placing the box in the outstretched hands of Raphael, he then proclaimed, "Now your soul belongs to me."

Raphael could not help but notice the ring on the finger of his benefactor, instinctively recognizing its symbolic meaning. Although he had not seen it before, he had known of its existence. The unmistakable carving of the cloven hoof was the true sign of the Prince of Darkness. Seizing the hand of Dracula, he fell to his knees, kissed the ring, and declared his loyalty and understanding of its symbolic meaning. He pleaded to be given the opportunity to serve. "And what is it that you want in return?" asked Dracula.

"To speak with the master," was his reply.

"Serve me well, and I promise you shall not only speak with him, but you shall see him," Dracula responded.

Thus it was arranged that Raphael Colonna would shelter and do the bidding of Count Dracula when he would subsequently arrive in the city of Rome to put his plan into effect. The plan was to make himself pope by proxy of the Roman Catholic Church.

The first pope was Simon. His name was changed to Peter by Jesus. Peter had made a great act of faith and for that was given the honor and responsibility of vicar of Jesus Christ on earth. Peter worked hard and well, until Nero struck out against the Christians and ordered that Peter be crucified. At Peter's request, he was crucified head down. He did not think of himself worthy to die upright on the cross the same way as Jesus. The place of execution took place on a hill called the Vatican.

Pope Leo X had been elected in the year 1513. Raphael Colonna, following Dracula's instruction, sought out Leo's leading opponent, a task that offered no difficulty. One, Cardinal Petrucci, was most vocal in his displeasure of the election of Leo. With a gift of two bags of gold, Raphael gained the full attention of Cardinal Petrucci. "You, sir, should be the one in the seat of power," said Raphael. Petrucci readily agreed. "Now, I have a houseguest with the solution to the oversight of the Electoral College of Cardinals in their failure to place you on the papal throne. Now if you would come to my villa this evening about eight, I shall introduce you to your benefactor, and over food and drink, we shall rectify their blunder. So I will bid you good day until this evening. May I ask if you have any objection to female companionship?" Petrucci smiled and then proclaimed in a loud tone as though he were addressing a large assembly, "It is our duty as well as our vocation to service our daughters, not only our brothers." Petrucci held out his left-hand palm down for the customary kiss on the ring finger indicating their meeting had come to a close. Raphael's first impulse was to spit on the outstretched hand but suppressed the urge. As an expression of amusement appeared on his face, he announced that he too was committed to a life of service. As he turned his back and walked away, Cardinal Petrucci was more than delighted, to say the least, at the prospect of replacing Leo with himself as the new head of the faith. He approached several of his fellow cardinals, who also were in accord with his spiritual as well as his political views. So overcome with sheer joy, his glib tongue failed him. As they queried him, for it was most unusual for him to display any emotion of joy, he shrugged off their inquiries simply by stating that they should make certain that they know where their loyalty lies.

Petrucci arrived at the appointed hour. He was taken to the study—a large room, thirty by thirty, dimly lit by two candles and a fireplace. He found Raphael standing by the roaring fire. At first, he did not see the other man seated some eight feet from the fire until his host announced that it was his pleasure to present his houseguest and benefactor, Count Dracula. The firelight cast strange shadows on the walls as Dracula left his seat and walked toward Petrucci. Extending his left hand, palm down, Cardinal Petrucci fell to his knees and kissed the outstretched hand. Why? He did not know. He felt somehow he was compelled to do so. As his lips touched the ring, he instantly withdrew in pain as his lips blistered. He felt that he had kissed burning hot coals. Attempting to recover his composure, he stammered as he looked into the eyes of Dracula.

"It is my understanding, sir, that you wish to aid me in my dilemma." When a reply to his question did not instantly come forth, he attempted to divert his eyes elsewhere as the fear of this man before him caused him to experience difficulty with his breathing. He began to perspire profusely. Aware and pleased with Petrucci's discomfort, Dracula smiled as he ordered Raphael to give wine to His Eminence. Dracula returned to his seat. Greatly relieved that eye contact had been broken, Petrucci turned to Raphael to accept the wine, which he drank greedily.

"To answer your question, you will poison Leo's wine. Raphael will give it to you before you leave. After you have accomplished this task, you shall have unlimited funds placed at your disposal to influence the outcome of the election in your favor." Petrucci was elated at the simplicity of the scheme. His fear dissipated, as he became overjoyed with the thought that he soon would possess the papal crown.

"I shall be forever indebted to you, sir. May I ask of what service I can be to you?"

"Through you I shall dictate the reconstruction or the order as it now exists. Now I suggest that we step into the dining room as food and entertainment awaits your pleasure." Seating himself at the huge table, he was awestruck as the five naked girls with ample bosoms entered the room and placed meat and fruit before him. Although he had been hungry only moments before, he abandoned all thoughts of food. After an hour of consuming several large cups of wine and fondling each of the naked young girls, who ranged from fourteen to eighteen years of age, he asked his host if he may be excused and directed to the bedchambers. He selected the two youngest girls to accompany him.

It was sunrise when he returned to his quarters at the Vatican. He slept until noon. So overcome with joy, he confided the plot to Cardinal Giulio, who he was quite certain was totally in accord with his own views.

Giulio, a cousin to Leo, thought for several hours of what had been revealed to him.

CHAPTER 17

PLANS AWRY

Before the pope's evening meal, Giulio had informed him of Petrucci's murder plot, and within one hour, Leo had Petrucci executed.

Not to be dissuaded by the turn of events, Dracula ordered Raphael to fully investigate the background of Giulio, confident that he would succeed Leo once he was disposed of. However, fate played a part, because although only fifty-six years of age, Pope Leo died unexpectedly one month after the execution of Petrucci. The origin of death has never been established; the date of death was December 1, 1521.

Dracula had almost guessed right in his assumption that Giulio would succeed Leo. After the death of Petrucci, Giulio was the dominant figure in the conclave but unable to control the necessary majority. He proposed a compromise candidate, Cardinal Adrian Florensy. His proposal was accepted, and Adrian was elected. He chose to be called Adrian VI. On September 12, 1523, he died, having been stricken with the plague.

It had taken Raphael a full year to gather the information Dracula required to put his second plan into play. Indeed, it had been a busy year for Raphael. His quest to fulfill Dracula's demand had taken him to Spain. It had taken him four months to travel to and from Spain. Finally, he completed the task and reported the information that he acquired.

Giulio De'Medici was born in Florence in 1478 and created cardinal in 1513. His slut of a mother died two months after giving birth to him. The father had taken him to a cousin, a pig, without a suckling of her own. The father, a Roman general, was killed in battle two years later. Ten years later, the woman gave birth to a girl. Giulio fell in love with the baby at first sight. The child was named Fantasi.

Giulio, at the age of fourteen, was told of his true parents; the news seemed to double the love he felt for those who cared for him and gave him love.

In the year 1513, he was elevated to the position of cardinal. A feast was given to celebrate the occasion. Fantasi was in attendance, and it was there that she met her husband-to-be, the ambassador to Spain.

They undoubtedly lusted for each other, for when he returned to his post one week later, they were wed. Tragedy struck, however, when a year later he was found dead in the stable, apparently the result of being kicked in the head by one of the horses. It is said that Fantasi was so overcome with grief that she took to drink; neither did she lack for companionship, as she took to bed all those who struck her fancy.

Raphael said, "I am sure you will be pleased to know that I have persuaded her to return with me with little effort, because she has squandered all that was left to her. I find it amazing she has retained her beauty and figure."

Raphael paused, waiting for a word or sign of expression that he had done well. Realizing there would be no such acknowledgment, he then asked, "What is it you will have me do next, master?"
Dracula replied, "Bring her to me." Raphael bowed and departed.

Entering the room where six hours earlier he placed her naked, in a drunken stupor, he observed the firm flatness of her stomach.

Her long hair completely covered her breast, which he knew to be large and firm; did he not have the delightful pleasure of undressing her? He had not taken his way with her, although he had more than a strong desire to do so from the first time he saw her. His eyes focusing on the huge mound of pubic hairs, he fought back the temptation of stripping off his clothes and seeking satisfaction. He had promised himself, the first day he saw her, that he would not possess her until Dracula himself had done so, thereby proving his loyalty and unselfishness once again and bringing him closer to the time when Dracula would keep his promise to arrange an audience with Lucifer himself.

Fantasi's eyes fluttered slightly, and with a low sigh, she opened her legs about eight inches, exposing the fullness of her womanhood. Realizing she was about to awaken, he dropped to his knees and put his lips on her, assuring himself that he was not compromising his promise. As he inserted his tongue into her, thinking that Dracula would never know, he convinced himself as he savored the wetness within. The blow to the back of the neck was so paralyzingly painful that he was certain he would never move from his present position. His dilemma was put to rest almost immediately as he felt himself suspended in midair and looking into the face of Dracula. "How dare you leave to your own pleasure before you do my bidding." The physical pain he felt was now displaced by the fear that gripped his heart. Not waiting for an answer, Dracula released his hold, causing Raphael to drop like a sack to the floor. After several seconds, he looked and saw that Dracula had left the room. He leaped to his feet and saw that Fantasi had fully awakened and was in a sitting position. He then took her by the hand and ordered that she follow him.

"Wait," she protested, "so I may cover my nakedness." Raphael forcefully led her through the door; instinctively, she knew any further protest would go unheeded. Soon she found herself standing in front of the fireplace, shivering somewhat and with her eyes downcast. She waited for the figure that she saw seated when she first entered the room. Raphael stood two feet behind him as Dracula observed her discomfort. He smiled as he left his chair and approached her; his eyes played over her well-formed body. She stood five feet three inches, one hundred fifteen pounds; her long straight black hair hung loosely, concealing her breasts. He looked at her face that was almost round, were it not for her oval chin. Her nose was slightly tilted upward, and her mouth was small, which was quite a contrast to her large grey eyes that looked at him inquiringly. He placed his hands on her shoulders and guided her into a full turn, gazing at the firmness and fullness of her buttocks. He made a mental note that her time with him would not be short or uneventful. Speaking in a soft tone, he asked that she forgive the ill manners of their host, turned to Raphael, altering his voice, and slightly demanded that he "bring a cape and food and wine for this lovely creature." Raphael, only too pleased to serve, went immediately to do as he was bidden. After she had eaten and drunk her second cup of wine, Dracula inquired about her comfort. Not waiting for an answer, he ordered Raphael to fetch quill and paper. Having written what she had been told, Fantasi was returned to the room and bed she had been taken from, but not until she had consumed several more cups of wine.

The hour was well past midnight, and Dracula, well pleased with himself, reread the brief note and then handed it to Raphael with instructions to deliver it to Giulio. How, he did not know, but Raphael mustered some semblance of courage to ask why had he been relegated to the position of a servant and messenger? As the hour was late, how was he to gain admission to the rooms that housed the cardinals while they cast their sacred vote for the new pope? It was well known to all that the rooms were sealed off from outsiders. The tone was low and icy as the reply to his questions came forth.

"You will bring gold and bribe one of those who attend to their needs, and he will be sure to deliver your message. Now, leave, or would you rather I snap your back like a twig?" During that brief exchange, Raphael thought that his life on earth had come to an end. He was more than grateful for the option given him as he bowed and fled the room that he knew held certain death if he tarried a moment longer.

Giulio was shaken gently; opening his eyes, he could not discern the face or the pleading voice hovering over him, asking to be forgiven for the intrusion. As he felt the paper being pressed into his hand, he strained his eyes in the soft glow given off by the oil lamp to see the intruder disappear into the shadows. He then focused his attention on the paper in his hand, with difficulty because of the poor lighting in his small cubicle. He sat up and leaned closer to the light on the table beside him and recognized the beautiful penmanship at once. Even before he read the first sentence, his heart skipped several beats. He was not fully alert as his mind raced ahead of his eyes, full with the memory of his dear and lovely Fantasi. Oh, how he missed her, he thought as he began to read.

"My dear, dear brother, although I must confess that I do not think of you as a brother now, nor have I thought of you as such for many years. Giulio, even now, as I see you through my mind's eye, my breast grows full with warmth, and I imagine what it would be like to hold your sweet face to my bosom and feel your kisses, but I know it will never come to pass.

"I am here in Rome, the guest of Raphael Colonna. He has been most kind, but I will not allow myself to intrude upon his hospitality. I have decided to be done with my life. When next the sun gives its light to the earth, I shall seek the refuge of the darkness of death by my own hand. I will not sustain my existence with the knowledge that I cannot possess you. When I put the knife through my flesh, my thoughts will be of you and the life we might have had. Farewell, light of my life." Signed, Fantasi.

Uncontrollable tears filled his eyes as he thought of his beautiful sister whom he had loved all of his life. How could such feelings have ever taken hold of her? But there was still time; he would have to break the rule of confinement and go to her at once.

A sense of foreboding befell him as Giulio awaited a response to his knocking on the door of the villa. Raphael Colonna asked of what service he could offer, pretending ignorance, after Giulio announced himself.

"You are aware, are you not, that I received a message from my sister, Fantasi?" said Giulio.

"I am, Your Eminence," replied Raphael, "it was I who arranged for its delivery, but not of its contents. I trust the matter must be most urgent to bring you at such an hour. Be good enough to follow me, and I will show you to her room."

As Raphael walked Giulio toward the stairs, Giulio crossed the open doors of a room that gave of lights from the fireplace within. He saw the figure of a man standing in the shadows. He only glanced briefly as he climbed the stairs and subconsciously reached into his cloak and touched the crucifix that he wore around his neck. Raphael, feeling somewhat foolish for rapping on the door, consoled himself with the knowledge that the need not arise again. Not waiting for an answer, he opened the door gently and stepped aside to allow Giulio to enter. "There is sufficient lighting inside, so if you will excuse me, I must see to the comfort of my other guest, whom you shall meet before you leave," said Raphael.

Fantasi, upon seeing Giulio enter, reached for something to cover her nakedness. She quickly left the bed to greet him before he had taken a dozen steps toward her, throwing her arms around him. He kissed her tear-stained face as she shook violently in his arms. Fighting for control, she whispered, "Giulio, what have I done? I prayed that you would not come."

Giulio replied, "I have come in response to your letter. I could not understand the folly of it; for you and I could not be closer if we were of the same blood."

"My dear, sweet brother, it was not my will to write and evoke your presence here, but that of the evil one. Oh, my brother, I have placed you in danger beyond words."

"I know," said Giulio, "though I cannot explain it, but I felt the abominable presence of evil as I approached the door of the villa. Dress quickly and let us leave this place. Do not fear, for the spirit of the Lord is with us." As they approached the door to safety, the omniscient shadow of Dracula loomed on the door before them. Dracula, realizing that his plan would not bear fruit, shouted obscenities and swiftly advanced toward Giulio and Fantasi. Giulio, sensing that he would be no match physically for the onrushing messenger of death, tore the large metal crucifix from his side. Dracula did not see what it was that struck him on the left temple, the shock of which caused his senses to lapse into a spiral void.

One hour after the rays of the sun had penetrated through the window of the apartment, one of many in the Vatican, Fantasi climbed into bed. She was two rooms away from Giulio's own bedroom. She was most grateful for the sanctuary that he offered and for accepting her vow of service to God and himself for the remainder of her life. Giulio returned to his cubicle; his absence went unnoticed.

Just as the sun gave off its last ray of light, the announcement came from the Vatican that Giulio had won the tiara. He took the name Clement VII. The following day, he sent twenty of the Vatican guards to the villa of Raphael Colonna, with the orders to put the torch to the villa and its contents. The captain of the guards reported back after the orders had been carried out, stating that when they arrived, they found a body identified by several of his men as being Raphael Colonna. They could not determine the cause of death, but it was obvious the body contained no blood. No one else was found dead or alive. Had it not been for his extraordinary foresight, Dracula would have perished at the home of Raphael Colonna.

Clement VII died on September 26, 1534.

Knowing that the pope would alert the citizenry and jeopardize his existence, Dracula sought refuge in France. In fact, it was there in the solace of his new confines that he realized that his powers must be increased. Therefore, he invoked the presence of his father of hades and prayed for the power to render fire harmless to him. As he prayed, he found he was momentarily encased in a ring of fire, and he heard a voice speak, "I hereby grant the sovereignty of the fires of earth." After receiving the baptism of fire, he immediately went into the city and claimed two victims. He was now certain he had achieved invincibility.

CHAPTER 18

NAPOLEON

He returned to France, processing an intellect that was incalculable. During the hundreds of years in his travels from country to country, he had mastered over twenty languages and developed a superb taste for the arts; after all, he had known the great and the near great of the centuries. For the past hundred years, he had also become more selective in choosing his victims who, unfortunately, were only the beautiful women. He ultimately also became proficient in the art of lovemaking. As his powers increased, he no longer had the need to continue his almost daily murderous attacks to sustain his life. He now required only one victim per week, and no longer did he mutilate his victims. He had developed the technique of puncturing the throat at the jugular vein, leaving only two small marks. This was virtuously painless to the victim. The attacks occurred only during intercourse when he knew the lady had reached the height of ecstasy. His motive was quite selfish, for he now understood that he could no longer leave a trail of mutilated bodies. He was aware of the police becoming more sophisticated in their methods of apprehending wrongdoers. More often, when the bodies were found, death was usually attributed to heart failure, and the few times the marks were noticed, they were thought to be insect bites. Thus his crimes remained undetected, at least for some years to come.

Having now ingratiated himself into the society of France, he gained the reputation of being a generous and elaborate host. On December 2, 1804, Napoleon Bonaparte was crowned Emperor of France. Count Dracula was invited to the coronation at Notre Dame Cathedral. He, of course, declined. He did, however, accept the invitation to attend the great ball held that evening at the emperor's palace. Dracula was presented to the emperor and empress. Josephine was delighted. This was not the first time the three had met. This was the second meeting between Dracula and Napoleon. The first was as guest of honor at Dracula's estate and an hour's ride outside of Paris. Napoleon did not wish to attend, but his wife had talked him into going. Dracula had given two parties that were the talk of Paris during the first three months of his arrival. Josephine listened as the ladies talked of the rich, handsome young bachelor who captivated the hearts of the ladies of Paris with his debonair manner, not to mention the lavish gifts he bestowed upon his guests.

Josephine became intrigued with the prospect of meeting him. So when the invitation arrived, asking for the pleasure of honoring them at his estate, she was delighted, but Napoleon was not so disposed. She reminded him that the coffers of France were in dire need, and perhaps so wealthy a man may be of some use to France. With mild reluctance, he agreed. One hour after they arrived, he praised and complimented her wisdom and insight.

No sooner had they entered the plush ballroom and introductions were dispensed with, Dracula asked Napoleon to accompany him to the study. Napoleon had difficulty accepting the invitation because he had taken an instant dislike toward his host for reasons he could not explain. He was in shock when Dracula asked him to do him the honor of accepting a gift of fifty million francs for France, or rather the equivalent in jewels. Napoleon quickly regained his composure and asked, "What can France do for you?"

"Only allow me to serve."

"Then, I thank you for France and myself."

"I will have my servants put the chest in a carriage when you are ready to leave," said Dracula. The two men then returned to the ballroom.

Josephine was completely captivated by her host as he spoke of the cut and color of clothes and of matching one delicate shade against another. He dresses with superb taste, Josephine noted with approval. He also delighted her with his witticism and gallantry. He complimented her endlessly, and as the evening wore on, she felt herself falling in love with him. The second meeting, prearranged, had taken place in her bedchambers one week later during Napoleon's absence. After several hours of lovemaking, he bid her good evening and departed with the promise of returning soon. It hadn't occurred to her to ask how he gained access to her apartment. Her only thoughts were of fleeting hours that he had held her in his arms, ever so gently. As he entered her, with rhythmical movement, he slowly brought her repeatedly to the state of exhilaration that she would not have dared dream to have existed. Unlike Napoleon's awkward attempts with his violent thrusts that caused constant pain, this man had brought her fulfillment and the realization of being a complete woman. As she lay in the oversized bed, feeling the warmth of his wetness between her thighs, she turned over as her own wetness mingled with his.

Josephine had been bedded by other men before. Napoleon was her second husband; she had married at sixteen. That marriage produced two children. Her husband, Alexandre de Beauharnais, at nineteen, was rich and good-looking. After four years, the marriage ended in a divorce. At thirty-two, she married Napoleon and, soon after, took on a lover, in fact two, but soon tired of them after realizing that it was she who gave satisfaction but received none. She thought it ironic that being considered one of the most beautiful women in France, it wasn't until Count Dracula came into her life that she obtained the emotional fulfillment that had been waiting to explode within her all of her adult life.

The clandestine meetings continued for several months during the absence of Napoleon, the last being two months before Napoleon was crowned emperor. As the evening wore on, Josephine waited impatiently for the opportunity to speak with him to inquire as to his whereabouts. He was quite pleased to note her anxiety, answering that he had been much preoccupied, but promised to come to her soon. She informed him that Napoleon would be visiting Italy in a month, but she would remain at the palace, adding that she could not wait that long and she would come to him. This, he rejected as being too dangerous. He then suggested that if he and Napoleon had some sort of working relationship, then his visits would not be suspect.

"Then you seek an official position in the government?"

"Not at all, my dear lady, I only wish to serve in an advisory capacity, because as I have spent many years in other countries, some of which were the enemies of France."

"I know so little politics," she said, "but of course, I will speak to my husband." He then asked to be excused, after having kissed her hand palm up, and departed. The smile on his lips as he made his way to the door was because his plan would soon be a reality.

His returning to France was for the sole purpose of ruling. For some time now, he had been thinking he should have his own country. Napoleon would wear the crown, but it would be he who would be the Emperor of France and, soon after, the world. Napoleon would be the extension of him for the time being.

As he approached the door, Etienne Clary, the son of General Clary, was attempting to force one of the two glasses of champagne into the hand of the beautiful young lady he had escorted. Louisa Purkinje, a Czech, had come to France to study at the University of Paris. At the age of seventeen, she had completed her studies and had lived with her uncle and his wife, Johannes Purkinje, who was in the employ of Napoleon. Johannes had booked passage for Louisa to return to her homeland, and she would leave in three days. She was most anxious as she wished to celebrate her twenty-first birthday with her family.

Etienne also had attended the university and had been her escort for the past two years at countless parties given in Paris. His greatest ambition was to have her surrender her virtue to him. He did, however, on one occasion, succeeded in having her fondle him in the carriage for a few minutes. After leaving a party one afternoon, he had gotten her to drink four glasses of wine and maneuvered her into a horizontal position. He suffered difficulty lifting the countless petticoats so that he could penetrate her with his manliness, and without warning, because of the intense heat of the day and the four large glasses of wine, fate struck a blow and preserved her virtue as her stomach ejected its contents. As the emetic dark-colored matter, for which he had been recipient, oozed from his face and down the front of his shirt, his erection quickly subsided, and he cursed his own stupidity for having given her so much.

Now realizing that this would be his last opportunity to induce her to stay the night, she explained that she did not love him and would save herself for her wedding night. She then implored him to see her home. Angry and frustrated, he cursed her and walked away. With tears filling her eyes, she blindly fled to the doors and out into the streets, bumping into Count Dracula as he waited his carriage. She excused herself and continued on. A few minutes later, she stopped, realizing that she was going in the wrong direction.

A black carriage pulled beside her, and a voice from within called to her by name, "Good evening, Louisa. May I be of assistance and share my carriage with you?" Somewhat startled, she looked and saw that it was Count Dracula as he emerged and offered his hand to help her in. Thanking him, she accepted. He was not a stranger to her for she had attended two of his parties and was quite taken with him. Louisa settled back as he asked her for address. He then repeated it to his coachman. Looking into her eyes, he said, "I see you have shed tears." Removing a silk perfumed handkerchief from his breast pocket, he dried her eyes and said, "Do you not know that one so beautiful should only shed tears of joy?" He then placed his hands on the sides of her head and gently kissed her eyes. He then complimented her on how beautiful she looked in her gown, stating red was his favorite color and also noting her courage in wearing one so revealing, exposing much of her breasts, which he assured were quite lovely.

He then placed his mouth between the cleavage of her breast and slowly moved his tongue. The feeling to her was electrifying; she had never before had a man speak words of such tenderness. She took a deep breath, which expanded the cleavage, and placed her hands on the back of his head, pressing him deeper into herself. Then she softly moaned as the hot substance rushed from between her legs, saturating her underwear.

They soon arrived at her uncle's home. He asked if anyone was at home. "Only one servant who had been ordered not to wait up for her return."

"Good," he replied, as he stepped from his coach and helped her. He then dismissed the driver and entered. After he closed the door, standing in the shadows of the dimly lit room, she became apprehensive. She looked at his face, and a sudden chill overcame her. She was about to ask him to leave because of the lateness of the hour when, without warning, he lifted her bodily in his arms and demanded the way to her bedchamber. Speechless, she pointed the way and, upon entering the room, desperately tried to regain her composure, mustering all her calm from within. As he put her down, she explained that she was sorry for her conduct in the coach, and as much as she would like to be made love to, she would not until she married. She then apologized again and asked in a much-firmer voice for him to please leave.

In an icy tone of voice that sent shivers down her spine, he asked, "Do you dare speak to me as if I were that weak idiot son of General Clary? You will disrobe and stand naked before me."

"No," she shouted, "and when my uncle hears of this, you will have cause to regret this affair." Nearby where Dracula was standing stood a table with a small copper bust of Napoleon. He picked it up and threw it, barely missing by inches the horrified girl. The bust hit the wall with the force of a shot and remained imbedded. Louisa then did as she was ordered. Slowly she began the ordeal of removing her clothing, after which she stood before him with eyes closed, thinking if she did not see him, the same would be for him. After a moment or two, he demanded she open her eyes. When she did so, she saw that he was naked as well. He was standing four feet from the door, and she suddenly realized that this may be the only avenue of escape. She bolted toward the door, but her effort was in vain. He took hold of her and threw her facedown on the bed. As he let himself down on top, he took hold of her outstretched arms, pulled them together, and held them in a viselike grip. "So you wish to save yourself for your wedding night? Have no fear; I will not violate your virginity." He then entered her anus. She screamed as her stomach cramped with violent pain, and a merciful darkness came upon her. The last thing she felt was his teeth biting into the side of her throat.

Louisa was found the next day by her aunt. The screams from the middle-aged woman quickly brought her husband into the room as well as the servant women. Noting the bloodstain between the dead girl's open legs, he asked his wife if she had moved the body. "No, I only touched her, and she was cold. I knew it was the cold of death." Johannes ordered that no one touch anything in the room. Surveying the room, he saw the bust of Napoleon imbedded in the wall, also, that her clothing was in a heap on the floor. This was very much unlike his niece, for she was extremely tidy. He then sent the servant to go for the doctor and the police and told his wife to fetch his kit, for this was a case of murder.

Johannes Parkinje, a Czech, along with his wife, left Bohemia six years ago at the invitation of General Clary, then Colonel Clary. Parkinje had once acted as interpreter during the Italian Campaign, and the two men became fast friends. It was Clary's suggestion that Parkinje could find a place with the French government when the campaign was over. The colonel also introduced him to Napoleon, and in the presence of Napoleon, he again made mention that France may have need of his services. After talking with him, Napoleon agreed. When Napoleon became first consul, he instituted the civil code and prefects. General Clary retired and was put in charge of police with the rank of colonel. He then hired Johannes Parkinje, bestowing upon him the title of scientific investigator. Parkinje had impressed Clary as well as Napoleon with his theory for the use of fingerprinting as a method of identification in crime detection. He had explained that the first recorded use of fingerprinting was by the Chinese and Assyrians for the signing of legal documents. To obtain a set of fingerprints, the ends of the fingers are inked and then pressed or rolled one by one on some receiving surface. He further explained that they may be classified and filed on the basis of the ridge patterns, setting up an infallible identification system. Most important of all, his research through the years proved that no two persons have exactly the same arrangement of ridge patterns, and they remained the same through life. Colonel Clary arrived along with the doctor and two assistants. Parkinje had just completed removing the prints from the bust of Napoleon as the men entered the room. They all offered their deepest regret, and as the doctor began his examination of the body, Colonel Clary asked Johannes, "Why do you think Louisa met with foul play?"

"Let me wait until the examination is finished," Johannes replied.

Fifteen minutes later, as the doctor washed and dried his hands, Clary asked, "Your findings, Doctor?"

"Well, she has been raped, but not in the usual manner. She still remains a virgin. There was a great pain, but it would not have caused the death. There is no doubt that she had a weak heart, so the pain and fear of the attacker, I conclude, were too much for her."

Johannes walked over to the bed and pointed at Louisa's neck and asked, "What do you think of this? Is it not strange that these marks have appeared on the bodies of several other young women and also observe the lack of color to the body?"

"I'll wager there is little blood left."

"Also the same with the other victims."

"I cannot account for that," replied Johannes, "but your observations are correct, even though she and the others were attacked in such a savage manner, I cannot explain the loss of blood."

"What is it you are trying to say?" asked Colonel Clary of Johannes.

"I do not know, but I want to be informed of the death of any more young women that have bite marks on their throats."

"Do you think the bite marks caused death?" the colonel asked.

"Yes, Colonel, but let us try a test. Doctor, here is a toothpick. Insert it into the wound." Having done so, the doctor replied, "I see what you mean. The jugular has been pierced, which would account for how the blood exited the body. But to where? Certainly the loss of so much blood could not just vanish or been washed away. The only signs of blood are the stains between her legs on the bedding."

"Then what is it we are looking for, Johannes?"

"Not what, Colonel, but who."

CHAPTER 19

THE PARKIJE

Napoleon and Josephine were having a late breakfast in silence until Napoleon lifted his head from his plate and asked, "What was it you were talking to Count Dracula about?" Somewhat startled, she feigned forgetfulness. She struggled to keep from breaking eye contact in the hope of giving the impression that she was to recall any such encounter with the man in question, recalling a quote Napoleon was fond of repeating—a good offense is better than a good defense.

"Oh yes, I am sorry. He gave me a message for you. How stupid of me to have forgotten. He wishes to share his knowledge with you concerning the adversaries of France."

"I am aware of his desire to be of service," Napoleon said.

"Will you speak with him?" she asked.

"He does not impress me as being a strategist in the art of warfare, but be that as it may, France and I are indebted to him. I shall summon him upon my return."

She pressed, "Why not before you leave?"

"Impossible, there is much to do before I leave." Wisely she elected not to pursue the matter. True to his word, upon his return, he summoned Dracula but was somewhat annoyed to learn that his messenger had been unable to contact him directly and had to return a second time whereby Dracula's servant informed him that his master could only be present during the evening hours and suggested that a meeting be held at 10:00 p.m. This coming Friday, three days hence, and if there was no reply, he would assume that his terms were acceptable. Napoleon was taken aback at the insolence and regarded it as a personal affront. He informed Josephine of his feelings of the matter, stating that he would not allow this upstart to dictate terms. "Please sit down for a moment," she said, smiling only with her eyes. As he looked at her face, all the anger quickly subsided, and she asked, "What is this power you have over me?" Now seated with her sitting on his lap and nibbling at his ear, she said, "Listen to my heart for the answer. You must know it beats only for you, now let us speak no more of Count Dracula for you may find that there is a reasonable explanation for his strange behavior upon his arrival Friday. Now, would you like me to make love to you? she asked, knowing the answer, for she could feel his erection as she sat on his lap. "How can I refuse you anything?"

At the appointed hour, Dracula arrived and was shown to Napoleon's office whereby he was cordially greeted. "Now, tell me, sir, how do you think you can be of assistance to France? Not that you have not been already, with your generous gift."

"If you please, sir, allow me to explain. Germany, Russia, and England are making preparations to wage war against France. Now what I propose is that you offer a peace treaty to the three, making the terms most favorable," Count Dracula suggested.

"And what makes you think they will accept?" asked Napoleon.

"They will understand that the treaty will bring peace to Europe." Dracula continued, "King George has ruled England the past forty years, and the sixteen years have been spent at war of which they have suffered a defeat by the American colonists. Their loss has been a grievous blow personally to the king, as well as to the English pride. Once you open the frontier, trade will begin, and they will prosper; that will soothe their wounded pride, and you will be looked upon as a great benefactor. Now, as England and the others enjoy their newly found peace and wealth, you will continue to build the largest army and navy in the world. Your war materials you can obtain from Germany, and when your fleet is of sufficient strength, you will attack America after which the African continent will be taken. Once this has been accomplished, the combined wealth and resources of the two will make France the most powerful force in the world, and then you will take England."

"But what of King George, do you think he will stand by while I wage war?" Napoleon asked.

"You do not have to concern yourself over the English king for he will be among the dead. Do you know that he suffers attacks of madness, and on these occasions, he must be confined in a straight jacket?"

"How do you know he will be dead?" Napoleon queried.

"I will see to it, after which it will be the first minister, William Pitt, who will be head of the government."

"But he hates France as much as the king and, therefore, will cause trouble."

"No," said Dracula. "We will remove him from the seat of power. The foreign minister, his cousin William Greenville, is an ambitious man who craves for the seat of power, so we will bring him over to our side. He, in turn, will hand over England; enough gold will see to it. After these things have been accomplished, the rest of the world will fall like leaves from a tree."

Napoleon was intrigued by all that he had just heard and was convinced that the scheme was workable, but he concealed his enthusiasm. Dracula sat, calmly waiting for an answer, his eyes boring through Napoleon, causing Napoleon to feel uneasy, but he forced himself to smile and say that he found it interesting and would think it over for a few days. "Oh yes, Count, I would like to know your objection to meeting during the course of the business day."

"I am sorry, but I am a creature of habit. It seems as though I only function during the evening hours."

"As you wish, for I too am at my best after sundown. Therefore, we will arrange future meetings at your convenience. Now, if you will excuse me, I have a desk full of documents that need my attention."

"Certainly, but I would like to present a small gift to you." Picking up the neatly wrapped package Dracula had placed on the table lamp when he had entered, he handed it to Napoleon, saying, "I understand you are a coin collector, so I trust you will find these of interest. Now I will bid you a good evening." Napoleon opened the gift and was indeed quite pleased to find twelve gold coins in perfect condition, bearing the likeness of Alexander the Great who conquered the known world in the year 336 BC. He was delighted, to say the least. They were already placed in a beautiful red velvet glass case, so he decided to leave them in place. He then decided to put them in the large glass case along with his other prized possessions. Opening the bottom door of his huge desk to retrieve the key, he noticed a franc note protruding form his case box. He knew he should not have been so careless and opened the box to find that several of the notes were missing. "So there is a thief among us," he said aloud. He rang for his secretary. "Summon Johannes Parkinje at once."

Jenean had just completed packing. She then placed the smaller case alongside the larger one on the floor. Then she smoothed on the blanket on the bed and looked around the small room to make sure all was in perfect order. Noticing that her books were not covered, she took a sheet from the dresser and covered them. As she did so, she could not help but wonder how long it would be before she could return to continue her studies. This small room had been her home for the past three years and would take her vows in one year. How happy she will be when the bishop places the ring on her finger and announces that she is the bride of Christ. She had thrown herself completely into her lifelong ambition—the study of anthropology.

She could not help wondering what could be important enough for Napoleon himself to have sent two messengers with a dispatch to the mother superior requesting that she be given leave of absence in order to return to France. She regretted that there would be no time to say good-bye to Father Bianco, her professor, who arranged for her to have access to the archives in the Vatican. He would often chide her, saying that she should have been born a boy, for she was the first woman he had taught who possessed a natural scientific curiosity. This would always bring a smile to her lips, exposing perfectly matched teeth. She was exceptionally tall, five feet nine inches, her weight never exceeding one hundred twenty-five pounds. She did have beautiful brown hair before it was cut off, which matched her brown eyes which always seemed to smile, causing her face to radiate. Yet when one looked into her eyes, it was clear that she possessed a high level of intelligence for her twenty-two years of age. Her thoughts were interrupted by the soft rapping at her door. She responded, saying, "Enter, please." It was the mother superior and one of her two escorts to take her luggage. The two women kissed each other on the cheek.

"Now you come back to us as soon as you can, my child, for there is much work to be done." With the faintest smile on her craggy face, she fought back the tears that were building up, but her tone of voice broke, as she ordered, "Hurry, you mustn't keep the gentleman waiting."

It always greatly disturbed her whenever one of her charges left for whatever the reason. She thought of them all as her daughters, but she realized in another three years she too must leave for she had already passed the retiring age. It was the help of her bishop that allowed her to stay until her seventieth birthday provided her health did not worsen. Be that as it may, the question on her mind was why she felt that there was something special about Jenean.

One week later, Jenean arrived at the home of her parents, and after a tearful reunion, she asked why she had been summoned by the emperor. Johannes was about to explain when he was interrupted by his wife, saying, "Please let our daughter rest. Can you not see she is exhausted from her journey?"

Johannes apologized for being inconsiderate and said, "I will speak with you upon my return, for I must go to my work." Jenean insisted that she was not that tired, but her mother overruled her.

"Now I shall prepare breakfast after which you will go to your room and rest. When your father returns, there will be time enough for talk."

Entering his office, he found a grim Colonel Clary waiting.

"Have you been waiting long?" Johannes asked.

"No, only a few minutes."

"I am sorry, but my daughter has just arrived, and she will be of great help to us."

"Have you told her of our situation?"

"No, I have not, but I will speak with her tonight about our dilemma, and tomorrow I will bring her here. Now I see by the look on your face that there has been another murder."

"I am afraid so, the fourth this month."

"Another young woman, I presume?"

"Yes, a lady of the evening. The body was discovered by her landlady about two hours ago. It seems as though the young woman was late with her rent. She knew that the girl was entertaining a gentleman friend because she heard them come in and go to the girl's room sometime after midnight. She opened her door so that she could see the gentleman leave, but by the time it became daylight, and he did not come out, she decided that she would go in and demand payment for a night's lodging. To her dismay, however, the girl was alone and quite dead."

"But what of the man?"

"She thinks he must have jumped out of the window, but I find it hard to believe." "Why? It is not so unusual for a criminal to escape by way of the window."

"I agree, but this was from the third floor, and upon examining the ground beneath the window, I found it lacking footprints, which surely would have been there if one had dropped from that height, which is twenty-four feet. In fact, there was a slight rain last night, and the ground was still somewhat muddy."

"If that is the case, then the landlady most certainly dozed off."

"Come, you can question her yourself. I have a man there to make sure no one disturbs the murder scene, so if you will get your kit, we can leave."

Four hours later, having completed his work and having questioned the landlady intently, he held firm the fact that she did not fall asleep while waiting for the man to leave. Colonel Clary watched as Johannes looked through his magnifying glass, matching the prints taken at the scene from previous murders. He put the glass down and answered the unasked question, "Yes, his prints are here." Colonel Clary seated himself into the nearby chair and said, "I am at a loss. We know the identity of this murderous fiend, but who will believe us?"

Johannes did not return home until after midnight, where he found his wife and daughter waiting. He apologized for the lateness of the hour and insisted that they retire for the night. Jenean was about to object, but seeing the strain on the face of her father who looked ten years older than his fifty years, asked, "Will you tell me tomorrow why I have been sent for?"

"Yes, tomorrow you will accompany me to my office, and then you will know all. Now go to bed and rest well for there will be much to do in the days ahead. Pray that God is with us."

At 8:00 a.m., Colonel Clary greeted Jenean affectionately as she entered his office with her father. After the adulation had been dispensed with, the colonel suggested that they get down to business. Jenean, at her father's suggestion, had shed her habit for conventional dress of the day. She wore a white scarf to cover her nearly hairless head, which she would not need in another month. Her head had not been shaved for three weeks now, and her hair was growing rapidly. Johannes was the first to speak.

"Jenean, the reason I have sent for you is because, aside from me, you are the only one with the knowledge of fingerprinting and its classification. Now to begin, we are faced with a series of murders that so far have only been perpetrated against young women. That, in itself, is not strange, but they all have one thing in common—all of the victims have lost a great amount of blood, and the only wounds found on the bodies were two small punctures on the throat. Aside from the fact that they have all been raped, we have come to the conclusion that the killer drinks the blood from his victims. Now there seems to be a pattern to his madness because there are four murders a month, once a week. It would seem that he has a need for blood. Why, I do not know. Colonel Clary thinks we may be dealing with a force of the supernatural."

"Pardon me, Johannes, but how do we explain the fact that he has eluded us when I and my men have watched his place of residence twenty-four hours a day, and still he manages to commit these fiendish crimes?"

Jenean interrupted, "Father, then you know the identity of the murderer? If so, why do you need me to help with the classification of the fingerprinting?"

"As you are aware, the science of fingerprinting as a method of crime detection has not yet gained acceptance and, therefore, would not be acceptable in the courts, and besides this, he is no ordinary man. He is, no doubt, the richest man in all of France. He also has the ear of Napoleon, and it is said that he has become the emperor's advisor."

"Who then, Father, is he? And how do you know that he is responsible?" Jenean inquired.

"A while back one evening, I was summoned by Napoleon. There was theft of several franc notes from his desk drawer. As I entered the room, Napoleon was admiring a gift—a collection of gold coins bearing the likeness of Alexander the Great. He put them on his desk and allowed me to look at them, commenting that he had always likened himself to Alexander the Great. He then told me of the theft and asked what I needed. I told him, after I had finished, I would need to check the prints of all who had access to his office. It was a simple matter. It turned out it was the cleaning lady, who quickly confessed. But fate, it seemed, had stepped in. I went to catch a thief, and I found a murderer. I took the prints from everything on his desk, which includes the case containing the gold coins. The prints I recognized almost at once under my glass. So the next morning, when I returned to the emperor's office, I asked who had given him the coin collection. He replied that it was Count Dracula. I was shocked, but I dared not tell him of my suspicions for I was sure he would not have believed me. I did, however, tell him of the murders, and then I asked him to send the letter to your mother superior, as I would need your help."

"Father, I know of this man, and I am afraid that Colonel Clary is right in his assumption. Count Dracula does posses supernatural powers."

The blood drained from the faces of the two men. Johannes was the first to recover from the shock of her statement, asking, "How could you know of him?" She explained that during the course of her research in the archives of the Vatican, she had come across a journal written by St. Francis of Assisi. "It is not common knowledge, but St. Francis spent a little time in Transylvania. Before leaving, he had written a log of the events that he had experienced. Most significant was his encounter with a Count Dracula." She then proceeded to give a detailed account of what she had read. She concluded by adding that the journal was given to Pope Gregory XIII by visiting monks from the monastery of Transylvania in the year 1585.

"Amazing," replied the colonel. "Then that would account for what I saw one of the nights I watched his villa with four of my men." He took a deep breath and, after pausing, continued, "In light of what you have said, Jenean, I would not have mentioned what I had seen with my own eyes for fear people would think me a lunatic. In reading the reports of my men on night watch, they stated that the surveillance was uneventful except that on three separate occasions, they saw a large bat flying from atop the villa. I thought it strange that they only saw one bat, for I know they travel in groups, aside from the fact that they are warm-blooded and would not be flying about this time of year. So I thought that my men may have been keeping watch with a bottle of wine or two. I, therefore, decided to keep watch with them. My first night there, I too saw the bat leave and return just before daybreak. Four hours later, after I had slept, I received another report of a murder of a young woman. So I decided to check all of the reports of the watch, and I compared them with each time a murder was committed, and I found that whenever it was reported that the bat was seen, a body was discovered a few hours later. If what you say is true, then that explains how he was able to leave without detection." "Well, thanks to my daughter, we now know how to deal with him," Johannes said.

"How is that?" asked the colonel.

"We do one thing. We do as St. Francis did—we contain him by placing a crucifix at the entrance of the villa, or we enter by force and destroy him by driving a stake through his heart."

"I am afraid not, my friend. As of this morning, the emperor has placed him under his personal protection. There are twenty armed soldiers guarding the villa with orders to shoot anyone who attempts to enter. If only we could explain this to Napoleon. Tell me, Jenean, if it is the same man, how did he manage to get out of the cell that St. Francis had sealed with the cross?"

"I can only guess that someone removed the crucifix—a thief, I would think."

Johannes closed his eyes, and one could see by the tightening of the wrinkles in his forehead that he was in deep concentration. After a few minutes, he opened his eyes and said, "If we gave enough proof, the emperor will have no choice but to believe us and thereby take action, and it is you, Jenean, who must do this. You must go to Transylvania and retrace his movements from the time St. Francis left. I am sure that once he had been released, the bloodletting renewed. Therefore, I am certain you will find records or documents, and while you are gone, we will do the same here."

"That is an excellent idea, Johannes, but it will take several months or longer, but under the circumstances, I guess there are no other options open to us. Meanwhile, this devil will continue to kill and feed upon our people, and we are helpless. I could, however, impose a curfew. When will you leave, Jenean?"

"Tomorrow."

"Good, I will arrange for your passage at once. Now I suggest you go and buy what you will need. I will give you a sufficient amount of money to take care of all your needs, and may God be with you."

CHAPTER 20

BETRAYAL

Dracula was very pleased because for the past four months, his plan was well on the way to success until he learned that Napoleon had allowed the churches of Spain, Italy, and France to reopen. On the evening that he discussed the matter with Napoleon and asked why he had done such a thing, Napoleon explained that he intended to bring democracy to Europe. Also, that he would teach the people to govern themselves, and that he would need the help of the churches to do so. Dracula lost control of himself and shouted, "I will tell you what those fools need."

Napoleon responded, "You are forgetting yourself, sir, I am the emperor." Looking at the anger on the face of Dracula, he suddenly felt his knees going weak. He knew his life was in danger and immediately rang for his secretary to announce that the gentleman was leaving.

Dracula secretly booked passage for England. Three weeks after his arrival, he gave the biggest party London had ever seen. He invited the nobility of England—four hundred in all. Of course, the first minister, William Pitt, was the guest of honor. Five hours after Mr. Pitt had arrived, Dracula informed him that the treaty Napoleon had sent was a plot and, if accepted, would allow him the time he needed to build the largest army and navy the world had ever seen, and then the invasion would begin. England would be the first. Thus, Dracula had set into motion the events for Napoleon to meet his waterloo.

Pitt thanked Dracula and said that he would call a meeting with his ministers to discuss this not unexpected development.

"Sir, may I make a suggestion?"

"Certainly," replied Dracula.

"I would be most appreciative of any input you may have to help us deal with this situation."

"Then you must respond with demands of your own," said Dracula as he continued, "first, he must withdraw his armies from Spain, Italy, Portugal, and Holland. Second, he must agree that there shall be no further build up of armament. Third, England cannot allow him to continue to rule an empire which consists of some sixty-five million people for fear of dictatorship, which endangers the whole of Europe. Of course, he will not agree to these terms. Fourth, you will insist, as a token of goodwill during the course of the negotiations, to preserve the peace of Europe. He will at least desist from further armament buildup. This, he will agree to. He, in turn, will make demands on you. Therefore, you will make a small concession or two. It will take about two years before the negotiations break down. At the end of that time, you will prepare to strike. Of course, in the meantime, you will be enlarging your own fleet, and victory will be assured."

Pitt asked, "Why do you have cause to believe Napoleon will agree to discontinue the build up of further armament?"

Dracula answered, "The French have been at work for many years. They are tired of fighting and dying in other lands, they have simply had enough. He will have to show that he is making every effort to preserve the peace for fear of insurrection."

"Sir, again I would like to thank you," said Pitt. "I find your suggestion brilliant, and I shall act upon it at once. Now I am afraid I have kept you away from your guests long enough. Now come, I would like to present my cousin, the foreign minister William Greenville."

As the two approached Greenville, he was engaged in conversation with the most striking young girl he had ever seen, and he was stunned by her loveliness. She was five feet six inches tall, although she appeared much taller with her raven black hair piled neatly to perfection. Her smile exposed white teeth. Her creamy white skin was void of any blemish. The beauty of her was only excelled by the radiant clarity of her deep-seated brown eyes that float in a lagoon of tranquility.

After pleasantries had been dispensed with, he took her hand in his, palm up, and kissed, slowly lifting his head and looking into her eyes, saying, "Your radiant beauty is most certainly a tonic to a friendless visitor in your beautiful country." He turned to Greenville and said, "Sir, I must congratulate you for having so charming and beautiful a young daughter."

"I thank you, Count, but I am afraid she is not quite as young as she appears. I know she looks to be sixteen, but Lady Isabella has just this past month celebrated her twenty-third birthday. She has yet to accept any one of a dozen suitors that have asked her hand in marriage."

Isabella interjected, "Father, I am sure Count Dracula is not interested in my lack of desire to choose a husband, and besides, Father, I have explained many times they are spoiled and dull-witted. But let us speak of things more interesting. Tell me, Count Dracula, of the latest fashions in which the women of France are indulging."

"Be assured, Lady Isabella," answered Dracula, "the gown you are wearing is by far superior to anything they have."

"You are much too kind, sir," she said.

"Not at all. The truth is the truth."

For the first time in his life, he had to admit to himself that he was experiencing a true feeling of emotion toward the woman. He thought to himself this must be what the stupid mortals call love. He found the feeling exquisite. He made up his mind that he would have her for his own, whatever the cost. Just to listen to her speak was like music to his ears.

"How long are you staying in London?" she asked.

"I am afraid that will be up to Mr. Pitt."

"I will call a meeting of Parliament tomorrow," interjected Pitt, "and I will put your suggestion to the floor. The answer shall be forthcoming in a week, and if I may press you into service, I would appreciate you taking our decision back to Napoleon."

"In that case, I will be leaving in ten days, Isabella," said Dracula.

"Will I see you before you go?" Isabella inquired.

Mr. Pitt interrupted, "I am sure that your father, in his position as foreign minister, will attend the negotiations in France, and I am certain you will somehow manage to persuade him to allow you to accompany him."

She turned to her father and asked, "Can I?"

"Well, if I said no, you would no doubt not let me go."

This brought laughter to the foursome.

"Now the hour is growing late, and we have kept our host from his other guests," said Pitt.

By 2:00 a.m., all had gone. Having paid the servants generously and then dismissing them, he too left and went to the slums of London where he found that which he sought. As his teeth penetrated the soft throat of the young woman, who had offered her services thinking she would earn a large sum, she listened to the sound of the blood being sucked out of her body; it was then that she knew the only payment she would exact was death. Leaving the neat little room of the dead girl, he vowed such a fate would never befall Isabella.

Eight days later, Dracula received an invitation to the home of the foreign minister. The other guests included Lord Camelford and his lady and the foreign minister's brother, the Marquis of Buckingham and his wife. He was useful to Pitt and Greenville because he controlled many seats in the Parliament. Also attending was William Windham, known at Eton as "Fighting Windham." Behind their poise and good humor, one fact weighed heavily on these men and their king—the defeat in 1781 by the American colonists and the subsequent loss of the thirteen colonies.

As they sat after a late supper, Dracula listened as they gave vent to their hatred of Napoleon. Pitt announced that war with France would be a war of extermination. Under no circumstances did the king want peace with France. Pitt said, "What the king feared the most was the fact that Napoleon had brought order and justice to France. Therefore, England may find itself involved in a revolution of its own if the idea proved attractive to their disgruntled subjects, to which all of the members of Parliament agreed." After another hour of small talk, Dracula thanked his host and hostess for a delightful evening, but not before exacting their promise that they would accept his hospitality and honor him with their presence at his villa for the duration of their stay in France.

Colonel Clary snapped the cover shut on his pocket watch and announced that it was 2:00 a.m. As he returned the timepiece to his vest pocket, he said, "Well, what do you think, Johannes? Should we call off the vigil? It has been more than a month since he has been seen. Also, he had not taken a victim during that time period."

"I do not know. If it were not for the guards," continued Clary, "I should think he somehow has left France."

"You are quite right, sir." The two men strained their eyes in the direction from where the sound of the voice came. Frozen where they stood, they watched as the voice took form.

"Good evening, sirs. I trust the night air is not too cool? In any event, I suggest that you return to the warmth of your homes to avoid catching your death of cold." Colonel Clary had seen men die on the battlefields of Europe, but now he knew, as Dracula stood within three feet of him, that death had a human form. It took all of his will power to break eye contact. Turning his head slightly, he announced in a clear, distinct tone of voice, "I am here in my official capacity as—"

Dracula interrupted, "I know why you are here, Colonel Clary, and you also, Johannes Parkinje. Your stupid efforts of surveillance of my person I find amusing. But now I no longer find your presence amusing."

"We are not concerned with what you find amusing," said Clary, "we have a legal and moral obligation to bring you to justice for your crimes. Your very existence is an affront to God and man."

"My dear Colonel Clary," replied Dracula in a voice that was barely audible as though he were questioning two mischievous children, "do you, dull-witted bastards, dare hope to think you can bring about my destruction?" Seeing the expression of hopelessness appear on the faces of the two, he knew his question rang true. Opening his mouth, he threw his head back and laughed, the sound of which sent shivers down the spines of the guards sixty feet away. Ceasing his laughter, he looked at the two men and smiled, "Come now, gentlemen. The wretched creatures I have taken were of no use to anyone. Only to me were they of service."

"What of the murder of my niece, you soulless creature?"

"Be thankful that I am sparing your lives tonight for if you continue to annoy me from this night on, I can promise, you and your family will quench my never-ending thirst." He turned and walked into the shadows.

"Can you see him?" asked the colonel.

"No, I cannot, but listen. Do you hear?" asked Johannes.

"Yes, the sound is unmistakable. It is the beating of flapping wings. Tomorrow we will know where he has been. God help the unfortunate woman tonight," stated Colonel Clary.

"Colonel, I do agree with one thing he has said. The nightly watch of the villa serves no purpose, so I suggest we discontinue doing so."

"I too agree, but tell me, Johannes, how do we fight this devil? I have been a soldier all my life, and I must admit, I am at a loss. While he mocked us, I wanted to take hold of him and strangle him. But instinctively, I knew any such action would have been useless and would have resulted in our deaths. I too felt that a physical attempt to overcome him would have been useless, but do not despair. At least we know who and what we are up against. We shall be in a better position to deal with him when Jenean returns. Until then, there is not much we can do except try and keep the women off the streets from sundown to sunup. So let us return to our homes. One thing more, Johannes, why did he not kill us?"

"I can only guess that he was aware we were not unprotected, and therefore, he would have been forced to expose a weakness." Johannes then took from his coat pocket a silver cross. "I strongly urge that you and your family get one each and keep it on your person at all times because in spite of what he said, I do believe he intended to kill us tonight. Have no doubt. He is clever."

Josephine expelled a sigh which clearly denoted that she was in a state of sheer exaltation. As he slowly withdrew his penis from between her legs, he kissed each of her nipples and then announced that it was time for him to leave.

"Can I not persuade you to stay? My husband will not return for two more days, and it has been so long since you last graced my bed."

"I am tempted, my lady," he said, "but I am pressed by time as I am expecting guests, and it will be necessary for me to give my undivided attention to their well-being. I will, however, call on your husband when he returns."

"I understand that your last meeting was most unfavorable."

"Yes, I am at fault, but I am sure I will be forgiven when I present him with good news."

Josephine replied, "Oh, he is no longer angry and is looking forward to seeing you again. He does value your advice, and he is also greatly pleased with the gift of the rare coins you gave him. That was very clever of you."

"Not at all, the coins are of no matter to me. Of all that he has given me, you are the greatest treasure, though he is not aware of it." He smiled and kissed her lightly and departed.

Count Dracula apologized for his outburst at their last meeting. Napoleon accepted and offered a glass of wine. The offer was declined. "Now tell me, my dear Count, your note said that you have a message from William Pitt. What do the English think of my terms for peace?"

"Most favorable, I can assure you," came the answer. "They are sending their foreign minister, William Greenville, to negotiate terms. If they are satisfactory, he will then submit them to Pitt."

"Excellent. When will he arrive?"

"Ten days from now."

"Tell me, have you been able to explain to him how grateful France will be for any assistance he may give?"

"Yes. He is quite aware that the gratitude of France pays off in bags of gold."

"You amaze me, sir," Napoleon said to Dracula, "you are a man of many facets." "I only wish to serve, sire."

"I will instruct my secretary to arrange for the very best accommodations for the minister and his staff."

"I have taken care of the matter. They are to be my guests. Now, sire, if you will excuse me, I will bid you good evening."

CHAPTER 21

JENEAN'S QUEST

"So, my child, you have read the journal of St. Francis in the holy city of Rome?"

"Yes, Father, and I would like to thank you for your time," Jenean told Father Avis.

"There is no need to thank me, Sister Jenean. I only wish to be of help. Ever since I received your letter a few days ago, I have been praying that somehow you were mistaken, but for what you have been telling me, I must concur."

Although he tried to conceal it, Jenean could see that Father Avis was visibly shaken. She felt a wave of pity for the little man. He stood no more than five feet one inch but a little overweight at one hundred forty pounds.

His jovial face creased with worry, and his gray eyes also reflected his deep concern.

"I am sixty years of age, and for forty of those years, I have been a monk, so I have never come face-to-face with evil, but tell me, how may I help you?"

"Father, I must learn all I can about Dracula if we are to rid ourselves of this creature. First, I must know how he escaped from the castle. Second, what he did afterwards, and third, can you help me prepare myself for the confrontation that will surely come?"

"To answer your third question," he said, "only you can do that. You must search your own soul. I suggest prayer, meditation, and fasting. As for your first two questions, there is another journal; this one was written by the local priest eighty years after St. Francis had written his. I have retrieved it from our archives because I knew you would be interested. Here it is. Now I shall leave you. I have duties that need my attention. Of course, you shall remain as long as you wish. I will see you to your room."

"Thank you, Father."

Jenean picked up the journal from the table and read the title, *The Year the Door of Hell Opened,* by Father Joseph Raymond. Four hours later, Jenean finished reading and then sat looking at the closed journal with tears streaming down her face, when she became aware of the presence of Father Avis.

"Come, Sister Jenean, it is time for you to have supper and rest." She dried her eyes and looked up at her host, not hearing a word he said. She took hold of his hand and gently pulled him down beside her. He offered no resistance, sensing her inability to speak. He picked up the journal and said, "I too have felt the pain of this remarkable man, and now you are apprehensive of the task that lies ahead and your ability to effectively dispel Dracula. Now tell me, have the writings of Father Raymond helped you?"

"Yes," she replied, "but I will have to reread the journal."

"But first you will have supper," Father Avis insisted.

"No, thank you, Father. I shall begin to fast, but if you please, I would like to have some water.

Three hours later, Jenean sought out Father Avis, explaining that she had finished and would like to be taken to the cave where St. Francis prayed. With reluctance, he did as she asked, strongly feeling that she should rest before beginning her fast, but also realizing that she stayed twenty-four days in the cave with only a little water. She ended her meditation and returned to the monastery. Father Avis was most happy to see her. He took her hand, led her to the kitchen, and served her a light breakfast consisting of a bowl of corn meal and fruit with hot tea. After the meal, they sat in the garden.

"Now tell me, my child, you find that which you sought?"

"If you mean, did I have a revelation, I am afraid not, but I have found a sort of inner peace."

"Then the written account of Father Raymond was of no help to you?"

"On the contrary, he actually had found the answer." She paused and looked to the heavens for what seemed like an eternity but, in reality, were only a few moments.

Father Avis could not contain his anxiety. "Please, Sister Jenean."

"I am sorry, Father, forgive me. Although I have the answer, I do not have the wisdom to convince the people to turn away from self-indulgence. You see, Father, mankind has created an atmosphere of force of evil around itself. Father Raymond's summation revealed that Dracula could not tolerate the opposite. During the time of St. Francis and Father Raymond, the villagers, on two occasions, united in prayer. In doing so, they eliminated what was conducive to allowing him freedom of entry."

"Then what will you do?" Father Avis queried.

"I will do as Father Raymond. He stated that after the unsuccessful attempt to take Marie from the rectory, which resulted in the death of the attacker, the people thought they were at last rid of Dracula. However, Father Raymond was suspicious because after all, no one could identify that burned body of Dracula even though he wore the crest of Dracula on his cloak. His suspicion was confirmed a couple of days later when word came of the discovery of two bodies almost drained of blood. The two men were sailors who were about to board their ship. Father Raymond also suspected that the dead man, thought to be Dracula, was also a seaman by the condition of his body. His left ear had been cut off. There were other sears of knife wounds. He, therefore, reasoned that the kidnapping attempt had been engineered by Dracula to halt any further search for him. Father Raymond then traveled to the seaport and inquired about the ships that had set sail before or after the discovery of the bodies of the two seamen. He learned that a Captain Manay, the master of the vessel *Lunar*, had left port after the bodies were found, and furthermore, a few days before he had been observed talking to a stranger of quality. He found out also that the dead man buried on the church grounds was a well-known rogue. Now convinced that Dracula had escaped, he returned to the village to make preparations to follow him, to the ends of the earth, if necessary, but it was not to be. Two days before he was to depart, Father Raymond came down with a fever which he, unfortunately, did not survive. This we know from the footnote of his journal written by his successor. So now, I must locate the ship's log."

"Where are you off to?"

"France, the *Lunar*'s home port. Father, I must leave at once."

"I am afraid that is not possible. Within two hours, the rains will come, and traveling down the Transylvania Mountains will be impossible, but the roads will be suitable for travel in four days. Now I suggest you rest and regain your strength for you will need to be strong of body as well as of mind."

"Thank you, Father, I shall do as you suggest," Jenean promised.

She sat alone for an hour, anticipating the journey home, and decided to take a short walk. Lost in thought, she stood at the edge of the cliff a hundred feet from the monastery. She had not noticed that the rock that was supporting her was slipping as a light rain fell from the sky. Then suddenly, the earth moved. She turned to step back. The effort was useless. A bolt of lightning flashed through the sky; her body dropped, fortunately, to the ledge twenty feet below. Had she been standing ten feet further down, the fall would have been a hundred feet. Again, under the circumstances, it was fortunate that one of the monks saw her walking in the direction of the cliff, and she was, therefore, found fifteen minutes after the fall. The monks, under the supervision of Father Avis, were adept in retrieving her broken body. It was found she suffered a broken collarbone. Both of her legs were broken; she had a fractured back and a brain concussion. Jenean lay comatose as Father Avis and Alex worked feverishly through the night. By morning, the two men had set the broken bones.

Alex asked, "Do you think she will live?"

Avis replied, "If I were a prophet, I could answer your question." Placing his hand on her forehead, he bit his lip. As he removed his hand, he said, "She is burning with fever. We must break it, or she will not survive the day. Quick, get blankets, Brother Alex."

Two days later, her condition was the same. The monks kept watch in pairs around the clock. On the third day, there was still no change, and the fever continued to burn the ever-growing weakened body.

Her weight was less than a hundred pounds, due to the several weeks of fasting.

The heavy rains had turned to snow. It would prove to be the worst storm in forty years.

"I have a thought, Brother Alex. Surely, she will die unless we break the fever. Bring me three buckets of snow. I will try to force more of the medicine into her." The medicine was obtained from the bark of several trees and crushed into a vegetable alkali quinine. He was successful, and when Alex and another monk returned with the snow, Father Avis had removed all the blankets save one. Several minutes later, Jenean was packed in snow. The two monks looked in awe.

"Surely, Father Avis, she will freeze to death."

"Let us pray, brothers."

CHAPTER 22

JOSEPHINE'S BANISHMENT

William Greenville's ship docked at 10:00 a.m, arriving with his daughter, Lady Isabella, and his staff of six. They were met by Napoleon's personal guard and escorted to the palace. They enjoyed a special brunch prepared for them, during which Greenville inquired as to the whereabouts of Count Dracula.

"I am afraid, sir, we will be deprived of the pleasure of his company, owing to his eccentric behavior of avoiding the daylight. In any event, the count will honor us with his presence this evening at the grand ball I have arranged in your honor, and then tomorrow you will be escorted to the count's villa."

Soon the conversation turned to Napoleon's campaigns, and he confided the secret of his success.

"The essential thing is to be afraid last." He told of his good luck in Egypt. He had once fallen asleep beneath an ancient wall that suddenly collapsed, but he awoke injury free, and he found in his hand what looked like a stone—a beautiful cameo of Augustus Caesar.

Josephine interrupted, "If you men are going to talk of war, I think we ladies should busy ourselves elsewhere."

As soon as the opportunity presented itself, Josephine whispered to Isabella, asking if she had found Count Dracula interesting.

142 · RAYMOND BOYD

Isabella smiled, "Would not any woman?"

Josephine agreed. Straining to conceal her jealousy, she pressed, "Tell me, my dear, do you find that you may have a physical attraction toward the count?"

"Would not most women?" said Isabella. Becoming somewhat annoyed, she added, "I can assure you, Empress, my virtue is still intact."

Relieved, Josephine apologized. "Of course, my dear, I did not mean to imply otherwise, but may I suggest that to avoid the risk of gossip, you accept our invitation and remain with us for the duration of your stay."

"I thank you for your concern," replied Isabella, "it is very considerate of you, but I have no fear of gossip, and I would not think of declining the hospitality of Count Dracula. I know that you are much older and wiser than I in matters of stately conduct, but I feel I can afford the extravagance of disregarding the no-nos of a hypocritical society."

Josephine, unable to control her hatred and with eyes blazing and through clinched teeth, uttered, "You are not the naïve, sweet child you appear to be, but a seasoned bitch." The two stood face-to-face for a few moments, wordless. A slight smile appeared on the lips of Isabella, but her eyes, in contrast, sent a wave of fear through the body of Josephine, causing her to falter as she turned to walk away.

At 8:00 p.m., Dracula came to the palace. He was the last to arrive, with the exception of Napoleon and Josephine, who came down from their apartment at 8:30. The music stopped upon the announcement of their arrival. Napoleon signaled for the music to continue. He then led his wife to the center of the room to begin the dance. Dracula danced for two hours with Isabella who seemed to be having the time of her life, which did not go unnoticed by Josephine. Isabella suggested to Dracula that he honor the empress with the next dance. She was furious and delighted at the same time as he bowed and asked for the honor of doing so.

As soon as they were somewhat out of earshot, Josephine told him that she was going to plead a headache and return to her bedchambers for a short while, and she expected him shortly after to make his way to her; she would assure Napoleon that she would be quite well in an hour after lying down and would return then.

Napoleon and Sr. William Greenville were engaged in light conversation as Dracula and Isabella approached. Isabella pretended to be hurt at the emperor's lack of attention, and as he complimented her gown, he stated, "Your loveliness has captivated the heart of every man present and the envy of every woman, and if the count does not object, it shall be my privilege to have the next dance."

"Not at all, sire, and with your permission, I shall step outside for a breath of air."

It was twenty minutes since Josephine had entered her room and stripped herself of clothing. As she lay full of anticipation, the nipples of her breast began to swell. Slowly she massaged them, and then, ever so slowly, her right hand moved toward her stomach until her fingers were entwined in her public hair. As she was about to release the warm substance within her, she was startled by Dracula's presence, and he asked if he might be allowed to assist.

"Why have you kept me waiting?"

Expecting an answer to her question, she was not surprised when after a few seconds, no explanation was offered, but instead he gently guided her over onto her stomach. The mere touch of his hand caused instant forgetfulness as she waited in glorious anticipation for his lovemaking that would temporarily unite them as one.

As he began the rhythmical motion, he spoke of times and places and worlds of gray shadows. Of these things she did not understand, but the melodic tone of his voice catapulted her somewhere between time and space. She cried out loud for him to join her. Suddenly, she was brought back to reality as his nails tore deep into the flesh of her shoulders. The pain instantly made her aware that she was free of the weight of his body. She gazed in horror as the large black dog leaped from the bed and out the open doors of the balcony. At the same moment, she saw her husband standing in the open doorway of her bedchamber. She reached for something to cover her shame, but her fingers were paralyzed. Nor could she find speech as Napoleon advanced to within two feet of her. In an obviously controlled tone, he stated, "Slut, you are to leave here at once. I never want to see your face again. Leave through the servants' quarters."

CHAPTER 23

WAR & MARRIAGE

Two days later, Napoleon summoned several of his generals and announced now was the time to make ready his plan to attack the English. When questioned of the peace treaty that was in discussion, Napoleon dismissed it simply by stating that he did not trust the English.

"But I shall continue to discuss terms with Greenville until we are ready to strike," he continued, "we must be assured of having Russia as our ally. Now the three countries that have had war with France in the past are Russia, Austria, and Prussia. I, therefore, have devised a plan to unite Russia and France. Marriage, gentlemen, is the plan; for there is no stronger alliance than it. Yesterday, the Ecclesiastical Court of Paris granted me an annulment. The details are unimportant. I have sent an envoy to St. Petersburg to ask Alexander the Tsar for the hand of his sister Anna in marriage."

After two weeks had come and gone, Napoleon became impatient that the tsar had not responded. He had counted on a speedy acceptance. Now he was sure that the tsar had prepared a refusal; in fact, a courier arrived a few days later with a letter confirming this suspicion. The letter was polite and brief. It stated, "Due to Ann's age of sixteen, any marriage plans will have to wait until she is a little more mature. The age of eighteen will be more desirable for further discussion."

Napoleon was not fooled. It was clear that there would be no marriage. He was disappointed that his plan had been completely disrupted, but being a superb strategist, he had an alternate plan. With haste, he sent another envoy to the Austrian ambassador to ask for the hand of Emperor Francis's daughter, eighteen-year-old Marie Louise. The request was accepted. Due to the loss of several provinces, after the last war with the French, Francis hoped that a marriage alliance would cause Napoleon to return them. To say the least, Napoleon was more than happy. He began at once to make plans for the wedding ceremony and her arrival.

Marie Louise had blue eyes, a rosy complexion, and small feet and hands. Her light blonde hair, which she wore in curls, gave her a delicate appearance. She was delighted with Napoleon's lovemaking on her wedding night, as he with hers. The results would later produce his first heir, a son.

Dracula, of course, did not attend the wedding ceremony but was present at the reception. Marie Louise was quite taken with Count Dracula, which did not go unnoticed by Napoleon. It was then and there that he made the decision to rid himself of Dracula. He somehow sensed that, given the opportunity, the count would seduce his young bride. He had long suspected Josephine had succumbed to the masterful eloquence of Dracula. Also, there remained the fact that he neither liked nor trusted this man who claimed his only wish was to serve France. Napoleon was sure that behind the pleasant exterior, there was, in reality, an ambitious and cunning individual whose ambition, he felt, undoubtedly equaled his own. In addition, although he would never admit to a living soul, was his fear of this man. Through a sixth sense, he knew he threatened his very existence. Napoleon motioned to one of the aides in attendance and told him to locate General Dumas. Within five minutes, he was before his emperor, asking of what service he may be.

"I would like you to ask Count Dracula to excuse himself from the lovely English lady and join me in my study. Explain that I shall only require a few minutes of his time, and be sure to offer the English lady my apology for the interruption. First, however, have seven or eight other officers present in my study before you escort him." He was confident that the presence of others would insure adequate protection from the one man he feared.

CHAPTER 24

LADY ISABELLA

J enean stood by the carriage that was to take her to the sailing vessel to take her home. Father Avis held her right hand in both of his. He looked deep into her eyes, and he said, "Surely, your recovery was due to the divine intervention of our Lord, for never have I or the brothers seen one return from the grasp of death."

Jenean smiled, looking more radiant than ever before in her life. The early morning reflected from her face as she replied, saying, "Yes, Father, I feel an inner strength that I have never felt before, and I would like to thank you for all that you have done for me."

"I am happy that God has allowed me to help you in a small way, to prepare for the task that lies ahead on the confrontation with the evil one that will surely come to you upon your return to France. Now go, my child, for there is not much time for you to board your ship."

"You wish to speak with me?" Dracula asked in a clear, low tone of voice that sent shivers down the spine of Napoleon and all else present as he entered the room. With slow, deliberate steps, he approached Napoleon, who was standing alongside his huge desk. As he drew within four feet of him, despite his efforts to remain calm, Napoleon was forced to seek refuge behind his desk as he feared his legs would not support him.

"Yes."

"Do sit down, sire, as you look somewhat pale," Dracula said with a smile upon his lips.

Drawing from some inner strength, Napoleon looked up into the face of Dracula but avoided his eyes, saying, "Sir, we applaud your generosity and your desire to be of service to France, but as you may or may not be aware, France is in dire economical situation, and there is much unrest, and I regret to inform you that the citizens have focused their displeasure upon you. The fact is, sir, they resent your lavish lifestyle." Beads of sweat began to appear on his forehead as he fought to find words to make his explanation seem plausible. He continued, "So I am afraid you have become symbolic of their hatred for the rich. Therefore, I have the unpleasant duty to ask you to leave France as soon as possible."

Placing both hands on the desk, Dracula leaned over within inches of Napoleon's face. Still with a slight smile playing on his lips, he replied in a controlled tone of voice that was audible to all present as well as menacing, "Do you think that you can dismiss me like some underling when I can take your life as well as these fools that you have brought in here for support and now standing here quaking in their boots? But I shall allow you and them to live, for it is I who shall sit on the throne and you who shall do my bidding."

Before Napoleon could respond, the youngest of the officers, a lieutenant and quite large for a Frenchman, at six feet five inches and two hundred forty pounds, summoned his courage and advanced toward Dracula, shouting, "How dare you threaten the emperor!" At the same time, he reached for the throat of Dracula. Now having turned, facing his attacker, Dracula, with a blink of an eye, raised his own hand and caught the would-be aggressor by his left wrist and yanked the arm from the socket. Before anyone could respond, the young soldier crumbled to the floor. They were snapped out of their shock with the slamming of the doors as Dracula departed the room. All eyes were now focused on the emperor Napoleon who had risen from behind his desk. The front of his britches clearly gave evidence that he had lost total control of his bladder.

The count seated himself at the table just as Isabella was escorted to him after her dance with Napoleon's personal physician.

"Please forgive me, Count, I could not resist the temptation of just once dancing during your absence with the lovely Lady Isabella."

"That is quite all right, Doctor," he replied, "but I believe the emperor has need of your services." He turned his attention to Isabella and suggested that they take their leave.

"Must we?" she asked with pleading eyes.

Unable to impose his will on her, he did not press her further. "Then you will forgive me if I bid you good evening? I will send the coachman back to await your pleasure."

"Please, Count, must you leave soon?" asked Isabella.

"I am afraid so, my dear." Taking her hand, he bowed slightly and kissed it.

He arrived in his villa three hours later after having claimed another victim. He saw that there were no guards.

"So that bumbling fool has withdrawn the guards, but before I am through, he and his weakling staff will replace those he has removed." He entered his quarters and became aware of another presence.

"So like a thief in the night you come to do murder, yes, Colonel Clary?" Stepping out of the shadows, the colonel replied, "The time has long since passed for you to join your master in hell."

Dracula responded with thunderous laughter. "And you have appointed yourself the avenging angel? My dear Colonel, you, like me, will not see the light of day." Dracula stepped forward. The colonel raised his right hand, exposing the crucifix. The effect staggered Dracula, causing him to turn his back on his adversary. The colonel then seized the opportunity to reach down and pick up a bucket, which contained approximately four liters of lamp oil. He then tossed the contents, drenching the black form before him. Then grabbing the nearby candelabra, he threw it at the feet of Dracula, and instantly, the oil substance ignited, engulfing the product of hell.

Anticipating the scream of pain, Colonel Clary was shocked beyond belief as the room became filled with the sound of laughter. He watched in disbelief as the flames smothered and completely died out, leaving his intended victim unscathed. Terrified with fright, he ran from the room and down the staircase and out into the night. About two hundred feet from the villa, where he had hidden his horse, he dropped the crucifix in his hasty effort to mount up. His heart pounded with fear as he rode into the darkness, only to be overtaken by the sound of flapping wings. His body was found eight hours later. The official cause of death was determined as heart failure.

CHAPTER 25

VON HELSING

The tall young man knelt by the single grave that contained the bodies of his mother and father who had met an untimely death exactly twenty-five years ago up to the day. This would be a day he would never forget, even if he had wished it. That day was a special one for him. The house smelled as though it had been transformed into a bakery. As he returned home from school, rushing into the arms of his mother, he asked, "Will there be lots of cake tomorrow, Saturday, for my birthday party?" Smiling, she asked of what party was he speaking.

Breathless, he replied, "Tomorrow is my tenth birthday."

"Well then, you are too old for parties and such." Seeing his large blue eyes begin to mist, she bent down and kissed him, saying, "Well, if you are a good boy and study your Bible lesson after dinner, I shall speak to your father. Now go and change your clothes, so I can finish my baking." It was her dream that her son would enter the priesthood one day, contrary to her husband's wish that the boy would enter the medical profession.

Heinrich Van Helsing was silversmith and a deeply religious man. He, himself, as a young boy, had dreams of becoming a doctor, but due to the accidental death of his father, he was forced to seek gainful employment to support his mother and his three younger brothers. His one sister, the firstborn, was perhaps the one most responsible for his desire to be a doctor. Due to her strength and bravery, although blind from birth, he never once had an occasion to hear her complain of her misfortune. He vowed that he would one day have a son that would fulfill his dream.

Thanks to his uncle, a master craftsman, he soon served his apprenticeship. Ten years later, at the age of twenty-four, he enjoyed the reputation of being renowned in the whole of Germany as the master craftsman in the art of silversmith. How sad, thought the young man as he knelt, that his mother at the age of thirty, and his father at the age of thirty-seven, should have been so brutally murdered in the prime of their lives. Speaking softly, he asked both for their forgiveness for having disappointed them. He had entered the ministry, but after two years of study, he could not accept the concept of "forgive the enemy" nor could he forget the vow he made to his dead parents at the age of ten to someday find and destroy their murderer. Had it not been for his mother's intention of surprising him and sending him to his cousin's home for the night, so she would be free to complete the arrangements for his party, he too would have met their fate. Also, she wanted his playmates present when he returned the following afternoon.

Their torn and bloodless bodies were found the next morning when the housemaid arrived, and although he did not see them, he was told of the condition of their bodies eight years later. He learned also that their fate was not unlike many others. He made inquiry of the police only to be told that they were at their wits' end and that the madman, after ten years of such attacks, apparently left the country or may have died of natural causes. This, he could not accept, but what could he do? Frustrated, he returned to school to obtain a higher education in order to qualify for and gain admittance to the college of medicine.

At the age of twenty-nine, he received his certificate of medicine. Now after six years of a brilliant career, he decided to abandon his profession and go in search of the murderer of his beloved parents. His decision to begin the hunt had been made yesterday in his office while treating a young, twenty-one-year old prostitute for a minor infection. She had just arrived from France. Observing her obvious discomfort as he began to examine her exposed lower body, he engaged her in conversation. He asked why she had left France at so pleasant a time of year. He was taken aback at her response. She explained that she feared for her life.

"How so?" he asked with a quizzical eye. Little had he suspected her answer would send him on the most dangerous mission of his life.

She related that a fiend was on the loose and committing murder, mostly it seemed on young girls in her profession. How many, she did not know, but several were friends of hers. He abruptly completed his examination when she asked, "Doctor, how was it possible for this fiend to remove blood from the victims without cutting them open?"

Looking at his pocket watch, he realized that there was little time left to go to the ship that would take him to France. His ambiguity resolved after so many years, he said a final prayer over the grave. As the dark clouds appeared overhead, he wondered if it was omniscient as he climbed aboard his carriage.

The ship sailed over calm waters. Jenean stood on deck at the side of the vessel, looking up at the countless stars while enjoying their majestic brilliance as they gave off their light to the heavens. Her thoughts were interrupted as she realized she was not alone. She turned her head slightly toward the stranger standing about five feet from her and saw that he too was lost in deep thought of prayer. Such was the intensity of the expression on his handsome face. His eyes were focused upward. Not wishing to disturb him, she decided to return to her cabin, but as she turned to leave, the rustle of her garments attracted his attention as she was about to walk past him. His eyes, no longer looking upward, were now looking into her own.

"Please forgive me if I have disturbed you, sir."

"Not at all. It was I who did not wish to interrupt your solace. Please remain. Permit me to introduce myself. I am Dr. Kurt Von

Helsing." Extending his hand, he smiled, and she too smiled and accepted.

"Jenean Parkinje, Doctor, and I do hope I have not disturbed you." While holding her hand in his, a strange sense of well-being came over him. Bending slightly to kiss her hand, a look of recognition befell him before he could complete the formality.

"Parkinje," he repeated the name twice. "Forgive my rudeness, but by chance, could you be the daughter of Johannes Parkinje?"

"Yes, he is my father. Do you know him?"

"No. I have not had the pleasure, but it is he that I make the journey to Paris to see, as well as Colonel Clary. Jenean, if I may address you so?"

"Of course, Doctor," she replied.

"Then you must call me Kurt." They both were aware of the naturalness of addressing each other by their given names.

"May I ask why you go to see my father?"

"I do not wish to burden you with my troubles. My story is not a pleasant one," Kurt said.

"Please, Kurt, it may help to discuss it."

Feeling somehow compelled, he withdrew his rejection and asked if she did not think too forward of him to ask if she would accompany him to his cabin. She complied without hesitation. He began his story, beginning with his ill-fated tenth birthday. By 2:00 a.m., he completed his story up until he boarded the ship. Without comment, Jenean related her own story. When she had finished, the sun had pervaded the small but comfortable cabin. Both now fully understood the naturalness of their acceptance of each other at first sight. Without further discussion, he arose from his chair and suggested that he see her the short distance to her cabin just ten feet from his own.

"Try to get some rest, Jenean. It is about six hours before we arrive at our destination. Following soon after, I'm sure our first encounter with the product of Satan will be at hand."

CHAPTER 26

ZANZA

Dracula awakened at sunset from his deathlike sleep. After dressing, he sat pondering his emotional dilemma, recalling the centuries of life that he had, but most importantly, were the endless years to come. He resolved that he would not remain alone. He must have Isabella to share the future with him.

A few moments later, he entered her apartment. She was standing naked, brushing her hair in front of the mirror. She saw his reflection as he stepped into the center of the room.

"Do come in, Count. I am sorry I did not hear you knock." Slowly and deliberately she walked to the bed and picked up the robe and gracefully slipped her well-formed body into it. "You wished to speak to me, Count?" she asked.

Somewhat surprised at her demeanor, he stepped closer, taking her hands in his. "Yes, I have come to offer you the greatest gift I can give," stated Dracula.

"And what might that be?" she asked.

"The continuance of your life," he said, "a life of eternal agelessness. Surely you have sense, my love. Just think, my darling Isabella, for a moment of what I am offering—an eternity of a youthful life, without the ravage of time to mar your beauty. You will sit by my side as the people of the world obey and serve our needs. And all this I will give you if you will give yourself to me freely."

Taking a step back, she gently pulled her hands free from his grasp, and as a slight smile appeared on her face, she asked, "How can you give me what is not yours to give?" As she slipped the robe from her body, she then reached for his hands and placed them on her breasts. "Do you dare take what belongs to the master, son from my loins?" She then filled the room with the sound of her laughter. A mask of hatred came over him as the realization of what she had said became apparent. Seizing her by the throat, he attempted to lift her body and smash her against the wall, but he was forced to release his hold as the flames emanated from her body. The agony of pain caused him to scream out.

"Zanza, why have you done this to me?" As he fled from the room, the sound of her laughter still rang in his ears.

Jenean arrived home mid noon accompanied by Dr. Von Helsing. Her mother and father were more than delighted to see her. After the formalities had been dispensed with, her father quickly told of the death of Colonel Clary as the continuance of the murders of the unfortunate prostitutes. By the time Jenean and Von Helsing related their stories, it was time for the evening meal, after which Von Helsing asked Parkinje if Napoleon had been made aware of the situation.

"No, but the colonel and I had decided to approach the emperor just hours before the murder of the colonel, though I must admit it was I who forced the issue to bring the monster to the attention of Napoleon, as Colonel Clary was most reluctant to do so. I guess it was his old soldier's pride of wishing to take command of a situation and charge forcefully and destroy the enemy. A very brave and dear friend. I shall miss him, and now Napoleon has left the country, and I fear for our lives, as I am convinced that monster will keep his promise to murder us all."

Von Helsing, who had sat quietly for some time, stood up and walked several feet toward the fireplace and, with his back to the others, announced in a clear and distinctive, low tone of voice, "We will not let that happen."

Parkinje was about to express his feeling of the hopelessness of the situation as Von Helsing turned and faced him. He saw, for the first time, the strength of the man that he had been talking to for the past eight hours. He could not explain, but by repeating the statement made by Von Helsing, his confidence had been restored. Rising from his chair, he walked toward Von Helsing and asked, "What is it we must do?"

"Go to him, but unlike the gallant colonel, we shall succeed, for we shall seek him out under the protection of God."

"Forgive me, Doctor, but what protection is there against this monster?"

Von Helsing turned his gaze toward Jenean. Understanding his meaning, she begged their indulgence and left the room. In a moment, she returned with an object wrapped in a beautifully woven cloth that she retrieved from her travel bag. Unfolding the cloth, she exposed a beautiful, hand-carved wooden cross. Her mother was the first to speak as she approached her daughter. She asked if her eyes were deceiving her.

"It seems to glow," she answered her own question.

"The Cross of St. Francis, Mother, was given to me by Father Avis the day I left the monastery. It had been retrieved from the castle of Dracula by Father Raymond." Turning to Von Helsing, Jenean asked, "When shall we begin our task?"

"Tomorrow at noon," he answered.

"Would it not be better if we left at daybreak?" she asked.

"Yes, but there is something else I would very much like to attend to first," he replied.

Jenean tried to comprehend his meaning, wondering what could be of more importance than the task at hand. Von Helsing took her hand in his and looked deep into her eyes and, after a pause of several seconds, turned his gaze toward her mother and father, who also had the same question in their minds.

Realizing their complexity, Von Helsing cleared his throat and stated, "Above all else, and with your permission and, of course, Jenean's, I would like to have her hand in marriage. I am hopelessly in love with you, Jenean." His eyes now locked on hers. His words were slow and deliberate. "I am well aware of your chosen vocation.

Had you taken your final vows, I would not have expressed my love for you. Please forgive me if I have acted with a lack of discretion."

Parkinje, with a slight smile on his lips, reached for the hand of his daughter and, looking at Von Helsing, said, "I speak, I am sure for my wife as well, in saying to you, that the decision is entirely our daughter's."

Breathless, all were now looking and awaiting Jenean's reply.

"I must admit your proposal has made me very happy. And I am in love with you. But I must have time to examine my conscience. It is late, and I suggest that we retire for the night. I will have an answer for you in the morning. Come, Doctor, I will show you where you will sleep, if that is possible."

Parkinje winked at his wife, as he led the way for the doctor. Shortly after, he looked in on his daughter and found her kneeling in front of her cross, deep in prayer. As he softly closed the door, he was certain that his child would get no sleep this night.

Isabella, her father, William Greenville, and their party set sail for England four hours after she left Dracula. Two hours after their ship departed, a violent storm erupted. The crew fought desperately to ride the storm out, but their efforts were in vain. The winds tossed the vessel from side to side into the endless walls of waves that it constantly pulled from the sea. Man and ship strained every fiber, but alas, the effort provided an exercise in futility as the vessel broke in half and sank to its watery grave along with its human cargo, save one.

The lone survivor, clinging to a trunk, was picked up by a passing ship. The captain invited her to his cabin, so she might change into dry clothes. She accepted and asked if her trunk could be brought to her. He thought it strange that nothing else had been seen afloat. It was even stranger that only her trunk surfaced, without which surely she would have perished.

He was about to mention what a great stroke of luck she had when she asked with a bright smile to whom she had to thank for her life. As she slipped off her wet clothing, all of his thoughts were instantly dismissed as he stammered, "Jones, Captain John Paul Jones II."

"Allow me to reward you." She moved close to him, pressing her naked body against him. She shivered ever so slightly as she pressed her lips to his ear and whispered, "Isabella thanks you and thanks you with all her body and soul."

Dracula surveyed the shambles of his huge bedroom. His anger now subdued, he pondered the question that took hold of his mind like a steel strap. Why had he felt pain as a result of the flames coming from her body? He soon reasoned that the answer could only come from his lord and master, his father, Satan himself. Standing in the center of the room, he softly asked if he had been forsaken. After a few moments had passed without a response, he screamed aloud, "I know you are here. I feel your presence." A sudden chill came over him. It rapidly increased. His body began to contort. The pain was unbearable. He attempted to flee, but he found his body would not respond. He was hopelessly frozen where he stood. A blanket of darkness filled the room. He could not distinguish which was greater, the physical pain or the coldness that held him in a viselike grip and deprived him of mobility or the fear that now possessed his entire self. As another blanket of darkness encompassed the room, a small flame appeared four feet before him, six inches in length and two inches above the floor. He attempted to speak, but the effort was in vain.

The flame began to grow until it reached a height of eight feet. It hovered before him as it slowly took form, the human form of he whom he had called. The brightness and heat that emanated from it did not penetrate the blackness of the room, nor did it radiate heat. His eyes could only see that which was before him.

"Prostrate yourself before me, you worthless dog." Not realizing how, instantly he obeyed. "How dare you aspire to place yourself in authority over the creatures of the earth? You, that are only fit to copulate with the swine of the fields. Are you not aware that it is I who mankind has worshipped throughout his miserable existence, although he is not aware, but by virtue of his greed, for wealth and power over his fellow man?" As Satan continued to speak slightly above a whisper, his tone reverberated violently, causing Dracula a constant flow of unbearable pain.

"The time will come when the mortals of earth will come to know that it is I who they must come to serve and pay homage, and not he, the so-called creator. So that you will bear witness to what I have said, I will allow you to continue what you will find to be your miserable existence. So you will know when the time is at hand for what I have said to come to pass, I will cause war after war, each greater than the last that will encompass every living thing in this world. And then man shall turn to me as the true god of the universe. Now, I will deal with you for your transgressions, your affront to me. For your indulgence in vanity, from this time forward, you shall cast not a reflection of your image. Also, as you are aware, you shall no longer have the power to thwart the pain of fire. The fact that you cannot venture into the light of day, lest you seek to destroy yourself, will serve as a constant reminder that you are not privileged to immortality. You will walk the earth to serve my purpose only. Henceforth, from this day, do not call upon me. Heed not my words, and when next I reveal myself unto you, so shall you suffer the damnation of the dammed."

Dracula looked on as the flaming figure slowly disappeared followed by the blackness that had pervaded the room. All that remained of the apparition was the hideous sound of laughter that echoed through the walls of the abode, the sound common to a family of jackals. Dracula returned to his normal state of being. Filled with fear and hatred, he resolved never to offend his master again. Although he was somewhat vulnerable, he still could enjoy the pleasures of the flesh. And did he not possess powers enough to overcome all that may attempt to challenge him?

Von Helsing waited in silent prayer with Jenean's parents, in the church, as she discussed her decision with the bishop in his spacious study not to take her final vows but to marry Von Helsing.

"Throughout the night I have searched my heart and soul."

The priest interrupted, "Permit me, my child. Has your decision lightened your heart?"

"Oh yes!" Jenean enthused.

"Then I see no reason to discuss the matter further. From what you have told me of Dr. Von Helsing, I believe your meeting was not by chance, but by divine intervention. It will, undoubtedly, take the combined strength of both of you to successfully complete the task you have undertaken—to rid this world of the parasite."

One hour later, Jenean kissed her parents good-bye, and then she and her husband drove off in their carriage, leaving her mother and father under the protection of the church. Turning to her husband, she asked if they would reach their destination before dark.

"The horses are well rested. We should arrive about an hour before dusk," he said, adding a smile to reassure her. With half the distance yet to travel, a mishap occurred. One of the wheels broke free from the carriage, the result of a snakelike crack in the road. They both knew that there was no turning back, although it would be dark now that they were afoot. As the last ray of sunlight disappeared from the sky, Jenean and Von Helsing arrived at the entrance of Dracula's estate. Instantly, they found themselves surrounded by a dozen snarling dogs. As the dogs advanced for the attack, Jenean unfastened her cloak and removed from her neck the crucifix of St. Francis. Thrusting it forward, she uttered the words, "Creatures of hades, return from whence you came." Instantly, they vanished in puffs of black smoke. Von Helsing immediately turned his attention toward the locked door. Removing a tool from his pocket, he expertly forced the lock to yield. Entering the darkened foyer, they quickly found lamps to light their way. As they walked about forty feet, they came to a halt as they approached the huge staircase. They saw a light shining beneath two large doors twelve feet in length and eight feet in width. Cautiously, they approached the doors and entered.

"Good evening," the voice said in a most friendly manner. "You are, of course, aware that this is your last night on earth?"

Seated at the head of the huge table, forty feet from where they stood, was the object of their quest, Count Dracula.

"Please be seated and help yourself to some fruit and wine." After a moment or two, they still had not acknowledged his invitation. Smiling broadly, he continued, "Come now, accept my hospitality and indulge yourself for the short time you have to live. I think it appropriate to call it your last supper. I can assure you that I shall indulge myself shortly. Starting with you, sir, and as for you, my dear, I am sure I shall find you most gratifying. Even now as I think of you standing naked before me, I am becoming aroused with anticipation."

Speaking through clenched teeth, Von Helsing interrupted. "On the contrary, it is we who shall bring an end to your career of wanton violence and murder."

Dracula lifted himself from the table and walked to within ten feet of Jenean and Von Helsing. The smile showed ever so slightly. His eyes locked with Von Helsing. It became increasingly difficult for Von Helsing to breathe. He realized that in a minute he would suffocate. With his last ounce of willpower, he reached out for Jenean's hand, who somehow had also been caught in the spell. But at his moment of contact, they broke free of the deadly force of his willpower.

Jenean began to recite Psalm 23. "Yea, though I walk through the valley of the shadow of death, I shall fear no evil . . ."

Dracula fell back a couple of feet, himself growing weak. He mustered his remaining strength and leaped. Simultaneously, Jenean tore the cross from her neck. The impact of energy that discharged from it caught Dracula in midair, throwing him back forty feet, smacking his body against the far wall. Shaken and filled with rage beyond description, he did not move for a moment or two. Jenean and Von Helsing took a few steps toward their adversary but were frozen in midstride as they observed the instantaneous transformation of Dracula into a four-legged beast. With eyes ablaze and foaming at the mouth, it gathered itself up and sprang at its would-be victims. Jenean was the first to react, taking four quick steps toward the onrushing messenger of death.

The horror of Dracula was apparently at the end. The doglike creature lay dead at their feet; the crucifix deep in its throat and protruding four inches from its bleeding mouth where Jenean had plunged it. Taking hold of it by its tail, Von Helsing dragged the carcass out of doors, his wife lighting the way. Finding only one spade, they took turns digging throughout the night. It was a step-down grave eight feet deep and two and a half feet wide. The light of day broke through the cloudless sky as Von Helsing climbed out, facing Jenean. She saw a look of shock appear on his face. Turning in the direction of his gaze, she saw that the carcass had returned to its human form of Dracula, the cross still intact, protruding from his mouth. Quickly recovering their composure, they lifted the body, dropping it into the grave. Von Helsing then began the task of shoveling the dirt into the hole.

"I know you are exhausted, dear; we shall leave this place in a few more minutes. There is something I must do. I will be back by the time you are finished."

Briskly, she turned and walked away. Returning in ten minutes, she saw her husband toss the spade as far as he could into the tall grass. Also, she saw that he had taken a team of horses and a carriage from the nearby stable. They were harnessed and ready. Taking her by the arm, he helped her onto the carriage. They drove off, not looking back. The flames and black smoke were absorbed by the endless sky, giving evidence of Jenean's handiwork.

CHAPTER 27

1809 AVIGNON

A city on the Rhone in Southern France had been the residence of the pope's during their exile from Rome in the fourteenth century. Kurt and Jenean Von Helsing moved there a month after the near-death encounter with Dracula. Life had been serene; Dr. Von Helsing had established himself within four months as one of the leading physicians in the city. Jenean gave birth to a son a year after their arrival. It had been agreed that if she delivered a girl, her name would be Jenean, and if a boy, his name would be Kurt. Kurt was a sickly baby from the moment of birth. The first two years of his life required constant care from his parents, and he became well and strong beyond belief. Now at the age of four under the tutelage of his mother, he was an able student. Jenean also thought it wise to tutor several other children free of charge. After the party to celebrate their son's fourth birthday, the illness of their son became widely known in the community. The mortality rate of a baby surviving an illness such as endured by an infant was one in twenty. Hence Dr. Von Helsing's patients largely were children. That evening after the party and before they retired, they both knelt in the small chapel that Dr. Helsing had built. Centered on the altar was a two-foot statue of the Virgin Mother and Child, and on the right side of this statue stood a one-foot replica of St. Francis of Assisi. Both were beautifully carved out of briar. On the left side of the statue was a three-foot marble sculpture of the archangel St. Michael overlooking the other two in a protective posture, with his right arm raised and holding a sword with outstretched wings. They both prayed in silence for about twenty minutes after which they looked in on their sleeping son, as they did so every night gleaming with awe in the joy of parenthood. Dr. Von Helsing was totally exhausted after a twenty-hour work day with the exception of one hour he spent at his son's birthday party. He was the first to slip into bed after which Jenean quietly positioned herself alongside her now-sleeping husband. The sense of foreboding pervaded her being, and sleep eluded her. Not wishing to disturb her husband, she gently arose and again looked in on her son. Satisfied that all was well, she then walked to the chapel where she prayed, asking for the strength to endure and overcome the horror that she knew was sure to befall them. Jenean remained there until the first light of day when she felt the gentle hand of her husband on her shoulder. His soft-spoken words inquired about what caused her to feel the need to pray. He told her he was acutely aware that he was alone throughout the night. She looked up and took hold of his hands and said in a tone of voice barely audible, "My darling, we must send our son away in order to save his life."

"Oh, come now, dear, why do you say that? Is it because you had a bad dream?"

Slowly rising, she put her arms around her husband, and as they stood face-to-face, he watched his wife's eyes began to tear. He immediately knew it had not been a dream that caused her to fear for the safety of their son. The next words she spoke sent shivers throughout his body. Just above a whisper, she said, "He is alive."

By order of Napoleon, the residence of Dracula had been demolished a week after Johannes Parkinje had given a verbal account by his daughter and Dr. Von Helsing of their encounter with the scourge of mankind, Count Dracula.

It was exactly 4:30 p.m. when Jenean thanked the last two children, along with their mothers, for coming to Kurt's birthday party. A hundred miles away, under overcast skies, were four men with picks and shovels digging the foundation for an army barracks.

As the sky blackened, one of them spoke, indicating that they should stop. He feared that there would be much thunder and lightning. The man working alongside him readily agreed. They had dug and removed seven feet of earth. The two men proceeded to climb up the ladder and carried their tools to the horse-drawn cart. One of them yelled to the two remaining men to stop working.

"Okay," was the reply. "You go ahead and leave, we will see you tomorrow." They were anxious for their fellow workers to leave because they had uncovered the skeletal left hand of a body. Attached to the hand was a large ring encrusted with diamonds forming the shape of a cloven hoof. The one who had uncovered it stared in awe, and as he did so, the other man stooped down quickly and removed it from the bony finger. An argument instantly erupted as the holder of the ring announced that he would no longer have to labor for the miserly few francs he was paid. He argued that it did not matter who found it; the ring belonged to him by right of possession. As he turned to leave, he laughed and advised his now-enraged coworker to continue to dig because he may find another ring for himself. He did not see the pickaxe raised and swung until eight inches of it protruded from the front of his collarbone. The attacker pulled back on the handle, causing the body to fall backward on top of the six inches of dirt that covered the bones attached to the exposed hand. As the pickaxe was savagely yanked from the body, the ground greedily absorbed the blood that gushed from the body. At the same instant, a bolt of lightning struck, paralyzing with fear the man holding the pickaxe. He saw the shape of a human body forming, and his eyes bulged out of their sockets as the blood in his body rapidly drained. The next day, it was determined by the police that a murder had been committed and that the other individual died of a stroke. However, two major factors puzzled the detective. One was that they had observed just two feet from the bodies a third set of footprints that they knew did not belong to the deceased because they had on shoes and the third set was shoeless. Furthermore, after the storm the previous evening, the temperature had dropped to twenty below freezing. What was baffling about this was that there were no footprints leading to the ladder. The question asked and unanswered was how did he leave the site? The medical examiner posed another question which was how was it that the stroke victim's body contained no blood? The police did not relate their concerns to the reporters that milled around the site.

A long figure stood in front of the imposing massive stone edifice of Notre-Dame, which was dedicated to the Virgin Mary. His right arm raised and his fist clinched, he shouted obscenities, swearing vengeance against all those mortals that did his bidding.

"My father rules the underworld, and I shall master this world." His rage was so intense that he did not hear the footsteps of the two gendarmes rapidly approaching him. "Who are you, and why are you with your cursing defaming the Mother of God?" Abruptly and without warning, the person to whom the two policemen inquired turned and faced the men and said, "You dare ask who I am?"

The policemen were frozen with fright from the sound of his voice.

"We are in the presence of Satan himself," the older of the two shouted.

"No, it is his son Count Dracula that you dare interrupt, you meddling fools." Immediately after that was said, the elder man was instantly killed. His body, with the limbs detached in front of the massive doors at 5:50 a.m., was discovered by the devotional that came to attend the first of several services held a day. The other policeman begged for mercy. Dracula's anger had now subsided, and his expression and tone of voice became congenial as he replied, "I will give you wealth in place of mercy if you agree to serve me for six years."

Taken in by Dracula's persuasive manner, along with greed, were motivating factors. With the assurance that his life was no longer in jeopardy, he readily consented. "Paul DuPont at your service, sir," he said, bowing as he introduced himself and then asked what it was he would have him do? Dracula gave him a sufficient amount of franc notes to purchase a double team of horses and carriage. He then drove to the former estate outside of Paris. Thereupon his arrival, he found his master waiting and was baffled by the fact that his master was alone and there was no sign of a horse. He pondered how it was possible for him to be here. Instinctively Paul DuPont knew not to ask. Dracula led him four hundred feet from the entrance where he ordered him to remove some shrubbery. After completing the task, he discovered a hidden locked door and was about to ask for the key when Dracula stepped in front of him and effortlessly pushed the door open. Inside there were two large chests and a bronze coffin. With the help of Dracula, he lifted the heavy cargo onto the carriage. Dracula was acutely aware that there was less than five minutes until sunrise when he would be placing himself into his place of refuge. Paul DuPont was instructed to drive to the French seaport of Marseilles. At sundown, Dracula emerged from within the confines of the coffin before his metamorphosis changed to a three-foot winged bat. Paul DuPont was told to take his cargo to a sailing vessel named *Mephistopheles* and remain there. The sound of flapping wings was heard as the bat took flight ahead of the galloping horses, causing them to break stride. DuPont felt his thorax tighten, cutting off his ability to breathe as he realized the apparition that he had witnessed. He knew for certain now that he had made a pact with the devil, for which he would not survive. Paul DuPont arrived at his destination twelve hours later, with a plan for his survival. As he pulled the horses to a stop, Dracula stood apparently amused as two policemen questioned him about seeing or hearing anything that would help in their investigation into the violent murder of the first mate of a ship that had docked less than two hundred feet from where they were now standing. Dracula assured them that he had not been aware of any disturbance, explaining that he had just awakened from a deep sleep. They had noted by his formal dress that he was a person of nobility, and such was their decision not to impose on him further, so they saluted and wished him good evening. Five sailors had been standing by when Dracula beckoned one of them and spoke to him briefly. Moments later, the men had removed the contents from the carriage and placed them into the ship's cabin. The men were unnerved at the presence of the six black wolves menacingly alert as the men placed the coffin and the two chests in the cabin. Needless to say, they did not tarry. Upon his return on deck, Dracula gave sailing instructions to Captain Renior, who moments ago had come aboard. The men recognized him and knew him to be a ruthless taskmaster. It was only the promise of triple wages to the seamen that prevented them from going ashore. The captain bowed as Dracula briskly turned and departed from the ship.

"At no time are you men to attempt to enter the main cabin. To do so you will forfeit your life. Furthermore, you will do your work in silence. We sail at dawn."

The crew had wished to enquire as to their destination but decided against asking, although they had reason since there was no cargo aboard except the coffin and the two chests that they themselves had carried onboard along with food supplies. Dracula sailed from Marseilles to Paris, back and forth, selecting his victims with impunity. The bloodless corpses were virtually disregarded because of the revolution that was in process. The first day of fighting, one thousand were killed, and in the following weeks, six thousand more had died. Throughout the country, the Parisian Revolution was generally accepted. The insurgence basically was ignited by the haves and the have-nots. Once peace had been secured, Dracula's bloodletting came under the scrutiny of the prefect of police, Louis Philippe. Unable to make use of his coach because the barricades restricted the movement of coaches, Dracula had been unable to be driven until the insurrection had been quelled. Paul DuPont, not available in the evenings to be at Dracula's disposal, enacted his plan of escape. He had covertly obtained a vessel by the name of *Savoir-Faire*. The crew of eight was not told of their destination until they were at sea. Furthermore, they had agreed with DuPont that they would not return to France. The proviso stated that at the end of the venture, they all would be wealthy men. The ship sailed at sunup. He had given China as his destination to the harbor master. Three hours later, the ship sailed into an isolated cove. There, DuPont had two of the crew change the name of the ship. A short time later, the lettering painted read *The Columbus*. As was promised, DuPont now revealed their port of call as America. Unable to locate Paul DuPont, Dracula was enraged and took the lives of a dozen gendarmes as they patrolled in pairs on their assigned post in Marseilles. After the onslaught, he sailed to Paris in search of Jenean Von Helsing. Jenean arrived in Paris twenty-four hours before Dracula. Her husband had taken their son to the Vatican and placed him in the care of the mother superior. He then, at his wife's insistence, returned to Avignon to take care of his patients at the home of her parents. Jenean expressed her concerns, stating that she believed that Dracula was alive.

"My dear child," her father said as he took hold of her hand. "Providence, I am sure, has sent you here. Only an hour ago, I was sent for by a messenger to meet with the prefect of police. As you can see, I was preparing to comply."

"Father, is it to do with Count Dracula?"

"I do not know, I was told it was urgent."

"I pray not," interjected her mother as she made the sign of the cross.

Thirty minutes later, Jenean and her father were being ushered into the office of the prefect of police, Henri Mangin. At six feet tall and a balding man of thirty-two years of age, he had spent ten years in the army. He swiftly rose in the ranks after five years and was promoted to the rank of captain in the tactical branch, where his keen mind stood in good stead with his superiors. He learned of the murder of Colonel Clary, whom he had served under briefly, a man he admired and respected and who motivated him to forgo his military career. General Andre Barbet retired and was appointed by Charles X to take over the administration of the city of Paris. It was he that Henri Mangin prevailed upon to be put in charge of the police because of their common bond, that being their friendship with the late Colonel Clary. He readily agreed and was pleased to be offered.

"I am pleased that the two of you have come to enlighten me."

"Sir," Jenean's father spoke, "my daughter and I can explain what it is that is responsible for the bloodless corpses that lie in the mortuary of Marseilles, as well as in Paris. I can offer scientific proof, and Jenean can relate her personal encounter with the fiend."

With an expression of deep concern, Mangin asked, "Who is it that we are up against, Mrs. Van Helsing, and who have we been unable to apprehend?"

Adjusting her chair, Jenean leaned forward and replied, "The question is, it is not who, but what?"

Obviously intrigued by what had been said, he implored for her to continue.

"I am going to tell you a story; it's a story of horror that has befallen mankind, and it's a story of the undead. He is one that must feed from the living by drinking their blood in order to maintain his godless existence. He is Count Dracula, the spawn of Satan." Ninety minutes later, Jenean gave a convincing narrative of her encounter with the immortal count.

"May I have a glass of water?" Jenean asked, after she had concluded her statement. Although there were several subordinates present, Mangin arose from behind his desk and walked the several

THE ALPHA DRACULA · 171

steps to the side of the room and retrieved from a table a pitcher of water and a glass. No one spoke as he poured and offered the glass of water to Jenean. It was he that broke the silence as he seated himself.

"I have two questions to address to Mr. Parkinje. You, sir, have stated that you have scientific evidence to further support this astonishing revelation as told by your daughter?"

Johannes replied, "Yes, sir, in my daughter's graphic account of the past events, it was decided that my participation would be omitted until she had concluded." As he continued to speak, Parkinje handed an eight-by-eleven-inch folder that he had removed from his case. Mangin removed from it a file card that displayed eight matching fingerprints. Clearly written was a notation of where they had been obtained.

Mangin studied them for a few moments and remarked, saying, "I must congratulate both of you for your tenacity. I also agree that the evidence is tangible. My second question is how do we proceed to eradicate this nemesis from God's earth?"

The carriage came to a stop alongside the gangplank. The coachman shouted, "May St. Christopher be with you, sir," as Dr. Von Helsing hurriedly stepped down out of the carriage, holding firmly his son in his right arm, and in his left hand, a valise containing a small portion of his son's clothing. The coachman's words were unheard. The swirling wind and torrential rain had muted his words. The storm had been raging for the past twelve hours. Von Helsing shielded his son as best as he could from the storm as he made his way up the gangplank onto the deck of the ship named *Faith*. Four hours later, the storm had abated, and Dr. Von Helsing fed his son two slices of bread, two links of sausage with cheese as well as an apple, and a cup of goat's milk that he poured from a flask. In a short time, young Kurt was asleep. Dr. Von Helsing decided to speak with the captain and inquire about whether or not the storm had caused much of a delay. The captain indicated that they were off course because the waters were very choppy. His estimate was that there would be about fifteen or twenty hours' delay. He then added that he was optimistic that should the waters calm along with a favorable wind, they would reach port no more than two or four hours late. As the two men spoke, a man approached, dressed in the garb of a high-ranking official of the church. Dr. Kurt Von Helsing was fortunate to have as a fellow traveling companion Jean Toulouse, the cardinal of Lorraine, who was also on his way to Rome. He was a jovial man of average height and a bit thin body. He appeared much older than fifty-four years of age. His eyes seemed to contain the wisdom of the ages, and his demeanor was robust.

"I trust that you, gentlemen, found the storm stimulating?" he ventured with a broad smile.

The captain was the first to respond. "I must admit I was quite busy, and I must agree that I did find it so."

"And you, my son, appear to be heavily burdened, is it not so?" he said, directing his remark to Von Helsing.

"You are very perceptive, Your Eminence," Von Helsing replied, his tone of voice and expression somber.

"Perhaps we should discuss what it is that has penetrated the essence of your being."

"May I suggest my cabin, for my son, I have no doubt, has awakened from his nap."

Upon entering the cabin, Von Helsing remarked, saying he was premature in his assessment because they observed that the boy was blissfully asleep.

"May I offer you a glass of brandy, Eminence, that the captain was kind enough to provide?" The cardinal declined, asking with Von Helsing's permission if he could except after he had been apprised of what calamity had befallen him.

Von Helsing felt it would not be prudent to indulge alone; therefore, he returned the brandy from where he had taken it.

"Before I begin, Your Eminence, I must say I was not aware that my troubled mind reflected my anxiety, but I am grateful for your concern, affording me the opportunity to temporarily unburden myself," He confided, even though he did not believe that the cardinal could do anything more than offer prayers. "I shall begin telling of my plight that has necessitated the decision to seek refuge for our son in the Vatican; my wife had a premonition, and as a result of it, we know that his life and ours are in mortal danger. I shall now explain why it is imperative." The cardinal listened impassively to Dr. Von Helsing's recital, and at the conclusion, having vividly recalled to memory the tragic events of the past, he was deeply apprehensive about the safety of Jenean. Exhausted, Von Helsing sat silently, anticipating the cardinal to vent skepticism of the events that he had related.

The cardinal spoke in a monotone; his eyes conveyed compassion. "Be assured, my son, the name Dracula is not unknown to me. How long will your stay at the Vatican, Doctor?"

"Two days. I have chartered this vessel for my return home." Von Helsing, overwhelmed with curiosity, pondered if he should inquire as to the cardinal's knowledge of Dracula.

"I believe your son has awakened and no doubt is ready for his evening meal. We shall speak later then, and I shall answer your unasked question. Now if you'll excuse me, I should very much like to be introduced to your son. Then I must retire to my cabin."

"Pardon me, Eminence, are you not excepting the captain's invitation to dine with him?"

"No, I have not forgotten. In light of what you have told me, I must forgo the captain's kind invitation. I shall now meditate for the next several hours. Please convey my apology to him. Come to my cabin at first light, and I shall tell you of my brief encounter with the son of darkness."

At daybreak, satisfied that his son would remain sleeping for several more hours, Von Helsing quietly departed from the cabin, and shortly thereafter, he stoically listened as Cardinal Toulouse related the event that marred his sensibilities. He had been on a hiatus in Rome when he received word to present himself at the Vatican to meet in private with the pope. He was given a task of the utmost urgency. In short, there was a conspiracy afoot to overthrow the dictates of the papacy.

"I was directed to confront an Italian named Orsini who, at the time, was thought to be the originator of the plot. The Catholic influence was objectionable by a significant number of disgruntled Frenchmen; ostensibly, he convinced them that France could not extend its sovereignty mandate by invading England and Russia. The resources netted would overflow the coffer of France, thus eliminating the poverty that the people had so long endured, had it not been for the intervention of the Sardinians prime minister, Count Cavour, for it was he who informed His Holiness. Napoleon III also was told, and he deemed it ludicrous. He voiced his concern of how such an undertaking could be financed. 'I myself, with all the resources at my disposal,' replied Count Cavour.

'No, it is impossible to engage in an endeavor of such a magnitude of what you have said; I have much more to occupy my thoughts than to be concerned that anyone would take his obtrusion wholeheartedly,' Napoleon III said. The pope knew that the Catholic question was particularly thorny, and he believed that any number of Frenchmen would not object to a military strike against the Holy Sea. The French army had not fully recovered from the Crimea Campaign. He believed that as long as poverty and upheaval existed, one such as Orsini could rally domestic opinion and give substance to his ravings. Although certain that Orsini, as well his ilk, would not succeed, but to avoid bloodshed, I was commissioned to seek out Orsini and persuade him that dire consequence would result in his unrighteous attempt to destroy the faith. I excepted the commission without question. I was furnished the whereabouts of his abode, and some hours later, at 6 p.m., I knocked on the door and a voice did bid me enter. I must admit a cold chill encompassed my person, and momentarily, I was paralyzed with fright. I could not explain it at the time, but I had the urge to flee. Instead, I executed the sign of the cross and proceeded to enter with abandon to my chagrin. What I did not know had been the fact that Napoleon had second thoughts. Only a few hours before I arrived, Orsini and a two of his accomplices were executed. I was greeted with a cordial 'good evening, allow me to introduce myself, I am Count Dracula, I see by your trappings that you have risen in the ranks; therefore, I conclude that you are an ambitious man. Tell me, sir, is not my assumption incontestable?' He stood there in the pale light of the room which was sparsely furnished, with a smirk of self-confidence. Surely, an imposing figure of a being. Instinctively I was aware that I would not be permitted to leave alive, especially if I did not agree to whatever it was he was going to propose. I could not verbally transmit what my feelings were at that moment in time. How does one describe what it is like being alone in the abyss with the visual presence of evil? I then became aware that I was being instructed to return to Rome and administer a sufficient portion of hemlock in the wine that the pope drinks during the celebration of the daily mass. My reward would be to sit on the papal throne and do the will of Lucifer. I knew I would succumb and obey. Suddenly, standing between Dracula and me was a figure of a being encompassed in an aura. At that instant, I became aware that my will power had been restored because his right arm was extended upward, and he held a crucifix. Dracula cowered and shouted with a voice that shook the foundation of the place we stood. An instant before his body vanished, engulfed in dense blackness, he said, 'Francis, you will not thwart me again.' My mind was completely numb. A moment after Dracula disappeared, I asked the heavenly being to whom I should thank. No reply was forthcoming, but just before he also vanished, I heard the sound of a multitude of birds chirping, and without a doubt I knew the identity of my benefactor. Now, my son, I see we have both been the recipient of the good graces of St. Francis of Assisi."

Von Helsing sat in mute silence; his senses overcome by a calm that was surreal. The experience lasted a few moments.

"Thank you, Father." Von Helsing immediately questioned himself as to why he felt compelled to thank the cardinal, although he was intrigued by what he had been told. He believed that the cardinal could do no more than offer prayer on his behalf. His skepticism was instantly abated by the pronouncement that he should be sure to come to the cardinal's quarters without fail before his departure. The subject of Dracula had not been broached again as they continued the voyage to their mutual destination. The ship, with the wind in its sails, blissfully glided over the once-turbulent waters, but alas, the fateful storm unbeknown to Dr. Kurt Von Helsing was on his horizon.

Mangin, prefect of police, with five of his top investigators, waited anxiously for the solution to the question of how to expunge Dracula. Their eyes morosely fixed on Jenean Von Helsing. The sound of laughter filled the room. They all looked to the sound that emanated from the rear of the offices, and as they did so, slowly, and in their disbelief, Dracula materialized.

His manner was not threatening, and his expression conveyed amusement as he spoke, directing a question to Jenean, "Do you dare, along with the fools here, to challenge my sovereignty?" In answer to his question, four of the men drew their revolvers and commenced to fire them. Suddenly, just as Dracula appeared, he disappeared.

"When next you see me, Von Helsing, you shall die, and the same fate awaits all of you for your complicity." The words spoken, although Dracula was unseen momentarily, overwhelmed the men; they all cast their gaze in the direction of Jenean. Mangin sat with his hands firmly clasped in front of him on his desk in order to keep them from shaking. The slight quiver in his voice gave rise to his state of nervousness.

Addressing Jenean, he said, "The question remains the same, Madam Von Helsing."

"Without doubt, gentlemen, we are facing a most difficult task. To your question, we must find his concealed resting place. His supernatural powers almost make it impossible to vanquish him in a face-to-face encounter. It will take all your resources to locate his hiding place; after which, a wooden stake must be driven into his heart."

"Where do we begin? Mangin asked.

"Paris is a virtual haven for one in hiding alone. If he is found during the daylight hours, he will be in his coffin where he must lie." Jenean then suggested that Mangin begin to analyze the logistics of the place, and most importantly, at the time his victims were discovered, if it had been determined that any of them were murdered shortly before sunrise.

"Then we must conclude that his abode is not too distant from the unfortunate victims."

Jenean continued her assessment, stating that she believed Dracula would savagely rape and carnage one or more unsuspecting souls just before he retreats to his place of refuge.

"Now, Messieurs, I shall leave you to your task. First, I would like to speak with you, sir," she addressed Mangin, prefect of police. The men, following the suggestion of their superior, assembled in the conference room. Jenean's father remained seated. "Please, Father, go with the others." Without objection, he complied.

"May I offer you a glass of sherry?" Mangin asked.

"No, thank you, it's very kind of you. I shall like to tell you why I had to speak with you alone. I did not wish to alarm my father; Dracula has marked us all for death."

"How much time do you think before he strikes?" Mangin asked.

"Forty-eight to seventy-two hours; once the search commences, he will not risk the probability that he would be found in his coffin; therefore, I believe he will exact his wrath on everyone he saw in this room. Furthermore, I did not wish to alarm my father that Dracula is sadistic. I am convinced that he will attempt to take the life of my father first and then your men, yourself, and lastly, my son, husband, and myself."

"Surely there is something that can be done to protect ourselves from this son of Satan short of finding him first. You have bested him in the past; surely you have not given up hope?" Mangin asked. "Also, may I ask that it was only a short time ago that he could have easily dispatched all of us, is it not so, dear lady?" Jenean pointed to the side wall on the right of the room where there was a foot-long crucifix.

"Did you not see the beam of light emanating from it? That is why he could not move toward us."

"Then we must arm ourselves, is that not so?" Mangin asked, his tone full with vigor.

"Yes, most certainly," she responded.

"We should go now to Notre-Dame and get crucifixes and have the bishop bless them. We shall leave immediately."

"Yes, do so," Jenean said. "I shall join you and the others a bit later. I would first like to write a letter to my husband and apprise him of the events that have transpired."

"I will have a carriage awaiting you," replied Mangin, as he hurried from his office to the conference room to gather the men to leave and make way the short distance to the Cathedral of Notre-Dame. Twenty minutes later, Jenean handed her letter to Mangin's secretary for posting. Moments later, as she stepped into the waiting carriage, a feeling of foreboding gripped her being. As she lifted herself in, the hand of Dracula reached in and took hold of Jenean by the throat and pulled her forward.

"Now is your time to die, you meddlesome bitch." With those words and without resistance he slowly squeezed the life from Jenean's body. Dracula's attempt to bite into her jugular and gorge her blood was prevented by a blue hue brilliantly encasing her. Dracula shrieked in pain of the damned as he released his hold on Jenean's lifeless form. Several of the policemen sitting by the windows were drawn by the unearthly sound that penetrated the building. Later, when questioned as to what they saw, the testimony by all had been a large black dog or wolf fleeing from the carriage. As several of the men hurried out of the building, the driverless coach, as if someone was holding the reins, quickly galloped away as the police were afoot in pursuit. Mangin, along with Jenean's father, Johannes Parkinje, and the others, exited the massive cathedral just as the horses came to a stop. A dozen in number surrounded the coach; all simultaneously came to a halt within two feet of it. The brilliance of the hue from within startled them.

Johannes Parkinje was the first to regain his composure and stepped forward and opened the door as the brilliance from within slowly faded and said, "My daughter's work is finished; she is with our Lord." Mangin, as well as the other men, came closer. He exclaimed, "Has one ever been so fortunate as to cast their eyes on a person so beautiful in death?" Mangin agreed with Jenean's father that she be taken home to Avignon to be laid to rest. The men that were in Mangin's office when Dracula appeared accompanied as honor guards. The cortege arrived five hours before the return of Dr. Von Helsing.

CHAPTER 28

THE VOW

With a promise from his son that he would be a good boy, Von Helsing kissed and hugged him. He then turned away quickly to avoid his namesake from seeing the tears rapidly cascading from his eyes. It took him twenty minutes to locate the guest resident, Cardinal Jean Toulouse.

An aide answered his knock. "Welcome, sir, His Eminence shall be with you momentarily. Please be seated."

"I assume your son is agreeably settled in to your satisfaction, Dr. Von Helsing?" stated the cardinal as he briskly entered the room," carrying a twelve-by-six-inch crucifix beautifully carved out of hickory and encased at the base with a one-inch relic bone from the body of St. Francis of Assisi. He handed it to Von Helsing, now standing gripped with a sense of urgency by the abruptness of the cardinal. The furrows on the face clearly indicated the given concern.

"Take this, my son, on your journey home and pray that you be given the strength of soul and body for the encounter. Now go and be assured that there is no jeopardy for your son." The ship bobbed, ensued by the storm that raged five hours before Von Helsing sat foot on deck. Although he insisted that it was unnecessary for the cardinal to accompany him to the ship, with a wave of his hand, Von Helsing's objections were dismissed. An escort of four men on horseback rode ahead of the carriage, drawn by two white matching horses galloping closely behind the escort on the abbyin way. By the time they halted on the wharf, the matching white pair was blackened with mud kicked back by the ridden horses in front.

The two men alighted, and Von Helsing implored, saying, "Please, Your Eminence, do not see me to the ship; get back into the shelter of the carriage to avoid your clothing from being soaked to your skin."

"No need to fret about my garments, my son; I only need a moment or so to extend my blessing on yourself as well as the vessel that will carry you to challenge once again the son of the dark angel, Satan." Von Helsing, without response, walked swiftly to the waiting ship.

"Is all in readiness?" he asked of the captain as he stepped aboard.

"Yes, sir," the captain loudly replied. The captain then gave the order to hoist the sails and cast off. A phenomenal event took place as Von Helsing looked at the dock. The cardinal of Lorraine knelt, and with his right arm extended, he executed the sign of the cross. Moments later, the storm subsided, and the ship faded away on still waters. At the gravesite, Dr. Von Helsing solemnly pledged that he would dedicate the balance of his life, and if necessary, his heirs, to eliminate Dracula. Mangin, along with his men, returned to Paris where the police were relentless in their search for Dracula's hiding place. Dr. Von Helsing returned to Paris one week later with Johannes Parkinje. He had divided his lucrative medical practice to associates. Once again, the men assembled in the office of Mangin, the prefect of police, to renew their strategy in the apprehension of the elusive foe. Several of the men expressed their frustration.

"Do not be dismayed, gentlemen," Von Helsing said as he arose from the chair.

"The vampire we seek has the cunning of the ages and his instinct for survival is incalculable." The men were in awe at Von Helsing's reference of the word vampire to Count Dracula. Von Helsing continued, "It is the blood of the living that is required for his continued existence; Dracula is a kin to the vampire bat that also sucks the blood from living creatures." A knock on the door interrupted the meeting.

"Excuse me, sir; I have an urgent message for Mr. Parkinje," announced Mangin's secretary as he handed the folded paper to the addressee. The message was brief; it was a request for his assistance in the baffling murder of five women who were all disemboweled. The medical examiner was mystified by the two puncture wounds on the victim's jugular vein.

"Please come at your earliest convenience." It was signed Charles Darren, CID (Criminal Investigation Department). He then handed the letter to Dr. Von Helsing, who in turn read it aloud, after which he made a startling announcement, "The vampire is in London, England. There is no need to continue the hunt. Parkinje and I must leave with all dispatch."

"Why do you say Dracula is in London? It's only six days past that another of his victims—the body still warm to the touch—an hour before sunrise was found," Mangin asked.

"I believe I have a logical explanation," responded Von Helsing. "Paris was the place where Dracula's attacks began. The attacks next occurred along the seaport of Marseilles. Now I will show you how I concluded my assertion." Von Helsing then removed from his inside pocket a portion of a map; he then unfolded it on Mangin's desk. "As you can plainly see, gentlemen, I have drawn two straight lines in red. The first starts in Paris to Marseilles, and the second in reverse. We know he cannot venture out during the daylight, and you may ask how is it possible to attack back and forth, leaving a trail of death. The answer, gentlemen, is he travels by ship." Still reluctant to accept Von Helsing's explanation, Mangin pressed on, saying that he had heard of the murders of the four just yesterday. He went on to say that it appears they all were killed on the east end of London; in fact, due to the violent nature of the attacks, the newspapers called them Jack the Ripper murders.

"Although I must confess, Doctor, that I cannot explain the punctures reported on the bodies."

Von Helsing slowly folded the map, and as he looked at those seated, he said,

"No doubt some overly imaginative reporter, not knowing the identity of the killer, has given Dracula anonymity a nom de plume. If you will, therefore, if there is nothing further, I think it best we leave for London where I am positive the quarry is afoot."

One of the men asked Von Helsing, as he and Parkinje were about to exit the room, "What about Dracula's threat to kill us?"

"If we are successful in his apprehension and destruction, none of you will have anything to fear. However, in the event we do not succeed, remember, time is his ally." The questioner was visibly shaken about the possibility that Dr. Von Helsing and Parkinje may fail in their pursuit of the fiend. They also were gripped with consternation. Three days later, Dr. Von Helsing and Johannes Parkinje were in the metropolitan police building, being appraised of the brutal murders by Charles Darren. After he had given a detailed account of the mutilation of the women, Johannes then stated that he had preserved the integrity of the last crime scene that was located on the second floor of a rooming house occupied by Catherine Leman, a prostitute, as were the other five women. "It is our hope that you, Mr. Parkinje, can obtain the fingerprints of the madman who is responsible.

"Yes, I will do my best, assuming he did not wear gloves," Parkinje replied.

"Then I suggest we proceed at once," the policeman said.

"I have a question, sir," asked the doctor.

"Yes, Dr. Von Helsing, what is it?"

"Have all the victims two puncture wounds on their throats?"

"Yes, Doctor, they do."

"Then we know the identity of the murderer."

"Tell me, Doctor, who is it.?"

"The punctures are the mark of Count Dracula, the vampire." Von Helsing gave a detailed account of his knowledge of the history of Dracula. Charles Darren, CID, listened in mute disbelief as Dr. Von Helsing unfolded his story. At the conclusion, Von Helsing proposed that they visit, as suggested by Mr. Darren, the boarding house and ascertain if there is a match to the prints that Mr. Parkinje has on the cards in his possession of Dracula. As suspected, Dracula's fingerprints were found at the scene of the crime. Darren informed the police commissioner, Sir Richard Mathews, and the home secretary, Sir Alfred Williams, about it, as well as Major James Halse and detective chief John Du Rose, CID. Charles Darren introduced Johannes Parkinje and Dr. Kurt Von Helsing. He then explained that it was he that had written, asking for the assistance in the apprehension of Jack the Ripper by means of a new method identifying a person by their fingerprints.

"I can assure you, gentlemen, that this new technique of identification is valid. As we all know, an eyewitness account of an event at best is fifty percent accurate; Mr. Parkinje has without a doubt identified the culprit as Count Dracula of Transylvania. But I must confess that the story he and Dr. Von Helsing related to me as impossible to believe. Their story defies one's sanity. Forgive me, had I not found Mr. Parkinje and Dr. Von Helsing's reputation impeccable, I would not have solicited their aid. Therefore, I believe Dr. Von Helsing should relate to you what he has told me."

Dr. Von Helsing slowly arose, and as he did so, he removed from his inside coat pocket the wooden cross that had been carved in the shape of a dagger and placed it in the center of the table. All eyes were instantly focused on it momentarily. He had accomplished the desired effect as they all gave their full attention to him.

"The perpetrator," Von Helsing began, "of the so-called Jack-the-Ripper murders was born in the year 1181." At the conclusion of his recital, Commissioner Sir Richard Mathews was the first to respond, indicating that it was preposterous, and directed his cynicism at Charles Darren, CID.

"What is it you hoped to gain by bringing us to hear this absurd tale of someone or something sucking blood to stay alive? I am sorry to be abrasive, but what I have heard here is a story to frighten children."

Major James Halse, ignoring Mathew's criticism, asked, "How do we go about the creature's capture, Dr. Von Helsing?" Before Von Helsing could respond, Sir Mathews announced that he would not waste another minute of his time listening to any more rubbish, and without further ado, he abruptly departed, vowing to see that the police would not waste their time in search of a myth. Pursuant to enact his threat, an unforeseen circumstance would cause him to tearfully apologize to Dr. Von Helsing the following morning at police headquarters as he related the heart-wrenching events that caused him immense despair. Overcome with emotion, he told of the trauma that had befallen him.

"I had fallen asleep in my study awaiting the arrival of my wife and daughter who had gone to the old Vic Theatre. I was suddenly awakened by the sound of flapping wings, and as I looked toward my bay window, I saw the devil himself hovering in the form of an exceedingly large bat. I sat immobilized. How long I remained I do not know. I was gripped with fear knowing that I was in its power. After it flew away, I still could not move for some time, and a strange sense of foreboding overcame me as I leaped from my chair. I was somehow compelled to rush to the front door, and as I opened it, to my horror, there lay the bodies of my wife and daughter with their throats torn open. I now beg of you, Dr. Von Helsing, tell me how and where do we begin the search?"

"Sir Mathews, we are now about to put a plan I have devised into action. I have concluded that Dracula's mode of travel is by ship," briefly Von Helsing apprises the distraught man standing humbly before him, before saying, "the plan is very simple; Major Halse has only a short time to leak out to a reporter that all ships in the harbor were to be thoroughly searched. Also, reveal the fact that I am assisting the police in their investigation, and that I have come to London because I know the identity of the fiend that has been given the name of Jack the Ripper." Johannes Parkinje and Dr. Von Helsing were provided a five-room cottage, courtesy of Charles Darren, outside Fitzroy Square on Court Road.

The search was scheduled for sunup the following day. The home secretary Sir Alfred Williams had insisted that the search of the ships begin at once. He relented after Von Helsing explained that by the time the men were fully organized, the sun would be down, and Dracula in all probability would not be there and would seek refuge elsewhere.

As the dark clouds slowly filled the void left by the sinking sun, a seaman hurriedly rushed into the police station, asking to see Dr. Von Helsing. When told that Von Helsing was not about, the seaman explained that he had an urgent message for Dr. Johannes Parkinje who was afflicted with a severe migraine, being grief stricken over the loss of his daughter and anxious and not properly rested in the hunt and destruction of Dracula. Dr. Von Helsing suggested that he retire and get some much-needed rest. Parkinje insisted that he could not rest until their work was concluded. Dr. Von Helsing instead offered Parkinje a pot of tea. Ten minutes elapsed, and the tea laced with laudanum brought about the desired effect. Oblivious to his surrounding, Parkinje peaceably slipped into a much-needed slumber. Dr. Von Helsing sat in the dim light facing the slightly ajar door.

Suddenly the door was unhinged by an unseen force, a pillar of dense smoke encompassed the door frame.

"I see you have been expecting my arrival, Dr. Von Helsing." Von Helsing watched and listened as the pillar of smoke slowly materialized into the dreaded being, Count Dracula.

"So you sit bravely waiting to join your wife, you meddlesome fool? I have grown stronger; your icons no longer deter me." Dracula proclaimed, as he took two steps forward. Von Helsing spoke, his voice crystal clear, devoid of fear, which stymied Dracula.

Before he advanced further, Von Helsing began saying, "Saith the Lord though your sins be as scarlet, they shall be as white as snow, though they be red like crimson, they shall be like wool if you be willing and obedient; ye shall eat the good of the land, but if ye refuse and rebel, ye shall be devoured with the sword." Von Helsing continued, saying, "Surely you yourself know that Satan is the father of deceit; your final reward for doing his bidding is a place in the abyss. Even he, if asked, could return to his creator. Therefore, I ask you to repent and denounce your ungodly existence."

Dracula's rage was restrained. As his face contorted, he replied, "You dare tempt me, you who were spawned from the dirt of the earth and was favored above my father and his legions? No, Von Helsing, my father nor I shall never succumb to your God. Now it is I that shall commit your soul to the abyss to wait judgment day. I shall tear that fool Johannes Parkinje's limbs out." Von Helsing quickly arose from the chair and stepped forward, his right arm extended; he confidently announced that he had something of someone Dracula had encountered in the distant past.

"You do remember St. Francis of Assisi?" Not waiting for a response, he stabbed at the outstretched hand of Dracula; the pointed tip of the cross penetrated. Dracula screamed in agony as the bone chip from the body of St. Francis came in contact with his flesh. Instantly, he felt his endurance ebbing.

"Have thou forsaken me?" With his left hand he took hold of Von Helsing's right wrist, and with a herculean effort, Dracula extricated himself. The force was such that Von Helsing was knocked back several feet, falling over the chair he had been sitting in. He did not see the metaphorical change into the large black dog from hell, as some people have described it, howling as it ran into the cover of the night. Momentarily stunned by the fall, he quickly recovered and ran as fast as he could to the barn where two horses and a carriage were housed. He saddled one and rode in pursuit of Dracula, unaware of the consequence of his plan to inform the reporter that a search of the ships would result in the capture of the killer. The plan was logical; the vessel that set sail immediately would no doubt be the one concealing Dracula. When it was printed that the Ripper was hiding on a ship, the people had been in a panic throughout the east end. A lynch mob conducted door-to-door searches. There were eyewitnesses that have seen two of the women talking to a man shortly before their bodies were found. He was described as over six feet tall and about thirty-four years old, also dressed in black, with a long black cape. Queen Victoria had been petitioned and in response expressed her confidence that justice would prevail. The truth was that the seven murdered prostitutes did not cause her sufficient concern until a member of the royal family met the same fate. Sarah Chapman, a fourth cousin to the queen, was found gutted seven miles from White Chapel. She also had been seen talking with a man of the same description only minutes before her demise. When informed that the assailant was hiding on a ship, the queen ordered a hundred soldiers to join in the hunt. She was horrified when told that the twenty-year-old and seven-month pregnant Sarah Chapman had been found gutted and the baby with the umbilical cord attached in the mother-to-be arms. A thick fog now blanketed the entire harbor. It was estimated that a crowd of three thousand descended on the docks where four hundred ships were moored; waving torches and lanterns, they converged like locusts, shouting and screaming death to the fiend. Dr. Von Helsing pulled his mount to a halt within fifty feet of the mob and, in a frenzy, tossed their torches; twenty of them rushed to the last vessel as they stopped five feet away. The devil dog, snarling, ran straight at them and knocking five of them down as it made its way on to the ship. The seaman that had asked at the police station to speak with Dr. Von Helsing stood with an axe and cut the ropes that held the vessel to the pier. His shipmates raised the sails as the ship broke free. The night breeze pushed against the sails, causing the ship to easily glide away from the hazard of the enraged would-be avengers and vanished into the bosom of the thick gray fog. All the ships were ablaze; burning embers leaped from the doomed vessels onto the pier and set it on fire. The crowd dispersed, and their own safety became paramount as the flames licked wildly about. At the conclusion of the melee, the sound of galloping hoof beats scattered those that were shouting obscenities; Von Helsing stopped two feet short of the edge of the pier and dismounted, removing his coat, and dove into the murky waters. With arms outstretched, he grabbed hold of one of the ropes that had been cut free from the dock. As he clung on, during the next two hours, he heard men crying aloud, "No, no, no!" It was followed by the splashing sound of bodies being hurled overboard. He listened as the distance of the splash helped him determine the distance where the bodies were being thrown. An hour later, the blazing sun dispelled the dense fog. Dracula, moments before, sealed himself into the confines of his coffin. The crew of five that had succumbed to their greed by expecting Dracula's promise of untold riches, now watched him savagely tear four men literally apart with horror. Now it was the sight of the fifth man, having been lifted off his feet with his legs spasmodically kicking as Dracula bit into his jugular, gorging the blood from him, after which the bloodless body was effortlessly tossed into the sea. The men then agreed they best abandon ship. They reasoned that while at sea, Dracula would thirst again, and one of them would be his victim. Also, it was decided that they would first lower the lifeboat and then break into Dracula's cabin and remove the treasure chest. They had no fear; they had come to understand that as long as daylight prevailed, they were safe. The conspirators busily attempted to break into the cabin and extract the booty. Von Helsing boarded the ship quickly and descended below into the cargo area, and there lashed to the side of the hull two barrels of cold oil, each containing fifty-five gallons. He then opened the spouts of each, and the liquid emptied rapidly. Von Helsing then removed from the shelf a lighted lantern. There was also a length of rope nearby that he soaked into the cold oil. He then placed it two inches from the floor on the bottom rung of the ladder and then set it afire. Hastily, he made his way upward and observed the men lowering the lifeboat. Quickly, he climbed over the side and lowered himself in. The looters were unable but determined to gain access into Dracula's cabin. In the next thirty seconds, their efforts would be moot as the bottom of the ship was engulfed in an inferno, and several moments later adjacent there were six kegs of gun powder.

Just as Von Helsing, with oars in hand, pulled forty feet away, the ship exploded, sending the brigand's to their ultimate reward. Dr. Von Helsing and Johannes Parkinje forty-eight hours later sat in the office of CID, Charles Darren. In attendance were the home secretary, Sir Alfred Williams, and Chief Detective John DuRose. Darren spoke, giving them a summation of the climatic results of the mob that ran amuck. The dead numbered—including those seamen that were unable to abandon their ship—were 352, plus 224 injured. In addition, five bodies drifted to shore, and sadly one of them with two punctures on his throat was the corpse of Major James Halse. On that somber note, Dr. Von Helsing and his father-in-law extended their good-byes.

Four days following the explosion of Dracula's ship, and one hour before sundown, a fishing boat returning with their catch off the coast of Ireland were attracted by the ominous sighting of currents moving a coffin directly towards them. Within minutes, it rested alongside the boat, as it bobbed; the thumping sound unnerved the twelve fishermen. Even so, they hoisted it on the boat.

THE END?

EPILOGUE

So as the seeds of the field must be nurtured and embraced by the soil to survive, truly so must evil be nurtured and embraced by mankind to survive. Ultimately evil will feed upon the embracer.

—Raymond Boyd

SUGGESTED READINGS

1. For a detailed study of the life of Saint Francis, read *St. Francis of Assisi,* by Morris Bishop.
2. For detailed description, see *Popes through the Ages* by Josheph Brusher, SJ.
3. For detailed description, see *Napoleon Bonaparte—An Intimate Biography* by Vincent Crodin.